Scattergun Smith

Scattergun Smith is not in the habit of leaving unfinished business. When he sets out after the infamous outlaw Bradley Black, his search leads him across dangerous terrain, and every fibre of his being tells him that he is travelling headfirst into the jaws of trouble. But Smith is like a hunting dog and will not quit tracking his prey.

Black has not only wronged the youngster Smith, but has killed innocent people, and has to pay. Scattergun is determined to catch and end the life of the ruthless outlaw before Black claims fresh victims. It will take every ounce of his renowned expertise to stop Black, and prove why he is called Scattergun Smith.

Scattergun Smith

Max Gunn

A Black Horse Western

ROBERT HALE · LONDON

ISBN 978-0-7198-1746-5

Robert Hale Limited
Clerkenwell House
Clerkenwell Green
London EC1R 0HT

www.halebooks.com

Typeset by
Derek Doyle & Associates, Shaw Heath
Printed and bound in Great Britain by
CPI Antony Rowe, Chippenham and Eastbourne

Dedicated to Chris, Matt and Jess

PROLOGUE

The tall lean figure stood mysteriously in the centre of the wide street. Smoke drifted across his awesome frame from a blazing barn at the edge of the town. Scattergun Smith pushed his coat tails over his massive holstered shotguns and rested his gloved hands upon their grips.

An icy stare in his poker face dared the trio of wanted men to come out from their hiding-places. Scattergun remained as steady as a totem pole and watched them as they spread out across the width of the street before him.

Dan McGraw had led his two brothers to the remote settlement in order to use it as a base. He had intended to strike out at the stagecoach lines as they transported strongboxes full of hard cash to payroll a thriving silver mine set in the hills.

The McGraw brothers had managed just one robbery when the fearsome and fearless Scattergun Smith rode in to town.

The blazing building had not taken long to be reduced to a blackened wooden skeleton as the fire at its core sent flames and burning cinders heavenward. The blaze had achieved its goal though. It had made the notorious outlaws emerge from their hiding-places.

Dan glanced to both sides and nodded at his siblings, Buck and Tom. The three men advanced towards the stationary Smith as he watched them.

'Who in tarnation are you, stranger?' the eldest of the brothers shouted.

'My name's Scattergun Smith,' came the reply.

All three of the McGraws stopped. Once again they looked at one another as though trying to gain courage from family solidarity.

McGraw leaned back and looked at the unmoving Smith from under his battered hat.

'Was it you that set this fire?' he raged.

Scattergun grinned. 'I reckon I might have been a tad careless with my matches, McGraw.'

Tom McGraw shifted sideways until his shoulders were against those of his elder brother. 'I heard tales about him, Dan. That critter is plumb dangerous.'

'Tall tales, Tom,' Dan grunted. He eyed the two impressive twin-barrelled shotguns hanging from a specially designed shooting rig on Smith's hip.

Buck spat a lump of well-chewed tobacco at the ground between them and squared up to the unholy figure.

'He's a bounty hunter, boys,' he said. Brown drool ran from his mouth and dripped on to the front of his shirt. 'I've heard that he's damn good with them guns of his.'

Dan McGraw could not comprehend what his eyes were looking at as he slowly slid his index fingers around his triggers. He had never seen anyone who remotely resembled Scattergun before.

'That *hombre* can't be any good at shooting,' he drawled. 'No critter that's half-decent with his shooting irons needs damn shotguns.'

Suddenly Scattergun Smith raised his arms to chest height and flexed his gloved fingers.

'I ain't hunting you boys, McGraw,' he told the three men. 'All I want is information. You provide me with that and I'll leave you be. Savvy?'

'What kinda information, Scattrgun?' Buck McGraw asked.

'Don't go talking to him, Buck,' Dan snarled. 'You can't do business with no bounty hunter. He'll start blasting as soon as we tell him what he wants to know.'

Scattergun levelled his eyes at the eldest of the McGraw men. 'Don't go getting your brothers killed just 'coz you figure I'm a bounty hunter, Dan. All I want is information about Bradley Black.'

'What kinda information?' Tom McGraw asked.

'His whereabouts will do nicely,' Scattergun replied through gritted teeth. 'I ain't after you boys. I've got a score to settle with Black.'

Dan grunted. 'He's lying, I tell you.'

Scattergun lowered his arms until his hands were just inches above the smooth stocks of his sawn-off shotguns.

'Don't go leading your kin to Boot Hill, Dan,' Scattergun warned ominously. 'I don't like killing at the best of times, but if you force my hand I'll surely oblige.'

The outlaws fell silent for the longest while as they mulled over the situation. Then the bull-headed eldest of the group snatched his six-shooters from their holsters. Within a mere heartbeat both Tom and Buck had followed their brother's lead.

The little town rocked as deafening shots spewed from their gun barrels. The trio of hardened gunmen fired their entire ration of bullets through the choking smoke at the strange figure.

Scattergun Smith had turned sideways on to his opponents as the red-hot tapers of death forged a route through the smoke towards him.

The tails of his long, loose trail coat were lifted as bullets narrowly missed their target. Then he drew one of his shotguns, cocked its hammers and squeezed them in quick succession.

Dan McGraw and his brother Tom were ripped to shreds by the buckshot. Large chunks of flesh and bone flew in all directions from their carcasses as dozens of lethal lead bullets tore them apart.

Buck McGraw had fared slightly better. The shotgun cartridge had caught him below his knees. His guns fell from his fingers as he clawed at his blood-soaked pants and fell on to his side.

The sound of spurs filled the ears of the last of the McGraws as Scattergun strode up to him and looked down upon his handiwork.

'Where's Black?' he asked. He ejected both

spent shells from the twin-barrelled weapon and then poked two fresh ones into the smoking chambers. He snapped the weapon back and cocked one of its mighty hammers.

Buck looked up through the smoke that billowed from the twin-barrelled weapon as it was aimed at his head.

'Why do you wanna know, Scattergun?' he asked, his fingers pressed against the exposed bones of his mutilated legs.

Scattergun did not reply. He pushed the hot barrels into the outlaw's face.

Their eyes met. There was no mercy in the icy stare of the man called Scattergun Smith.

'He's headed to a town called San Miguel,' Buck answered Smith at last.

'How come?'

'Some rich critter has hired his filthy hide.' McGraw coughed wearily. 'He left here yesterday on the stagecoach trail.'

'I know a short cut. I ought to be able to catch up with Black long before he reaches San Miguel,' Scattergun said thoughtfully. 'I'll head across Dry Gulch and cut a whole day off the journey.'

Scattergun pushed the hefty weapon into its holster and turned on his heel. Buck McGraw watched in agony as the tall figure vanished into the clouds of smoke that still rose from the burning building.

'I still reckon you're a stinking bounty hunter,' he whispered painfully.

ONE

Bradley Black ran his gloved hand down the neck of his exhausted grey gelding and stared at the cluster of buildings before him. Although the settlement seemed hardly large enough to be considered a town, it nevertheless boasted a saloon. The infamous outlaw rubbed the sweat off on to his greasy pants' leg, then his eyes narrowed. There were three horses tied up outside the saloon; he was only expecting two.

Black slapped the horse and rode slowly across the sunbaked sand towards the saloon. With every step his eyes darted around the scattering of buildings; then, briefly, he cast his gaze back along the way he had come.

He drew rein when he reached the drinking

hole and was about to dismount when he glimpsed something out on the prairie behind him.

Black rose in his stirrups. He balanced for a few moments, chewing on the half-spent cigar in his mouth. *The rider was still following*, he told himself silently.

He could see the sun catching the horseman's weaponry and saddle trimmings. The outlaw's mind raced as he lowered himself back down on to his saddle.

'That critter's bin dogging my tail for too long,' he mumbled. He threw his leg over his saddle cantle and dropped to the ground. He spat the cigar to the ground, then looped his leathers over the hitching-pole and secured them.

Black stepped up on to the boardwalk, pushed the swing doors of the saloon apart and entered. He waited while the doors kept rocking on their hinges and his eyes adjusted to the darker interior of the saloon.

A score of flies buzzed around the trail-weary man as he strode across the sawdust-covered floor. Reaching the long bar counter he placed his left hand upon it while his right hand rested on his pearl-handled .45.

The bartender was fat and old, yet he still waxed

his handlebar moustache. Black pointed at a bottle and tossed a coin at the man.

As he waited for the ancient barkeep to deliver his whiskey, Black stared into the mirror which faced him. His eyes sped from one face to another before they lit upon the two young gunmen he had telegraphed to meet him here.

The bartender filled a glass with whiskey. Black gripped it and then noticed the pair rise from their chairs and start towards him. He downed the hard liquor, placed the glass down and pushed it forward. The bartender knew exactly what Black silently wanted, so he refilled the glass.

Black was about to pick up the glass again when his keen eyes noticed the reflection of a seated figure in the wall mirror. He was sitting, masked by shadow, in the corner of the nameless saloon. The reflection was not clear and Black could not identify the man, but something warned the ruthless killer that trouble was brewing.

As the two young guns reached the counter they split and went to either side of the notorious outlaw. Black ignored them and kept his eyes firmly on the man in the corner. Every stinking hair on the nape of his neck tingled.

'Howdy, Brad,' one of the young guns said to

Black in cheerful greeting.

Black did not utter a word. He was watching the reflection of the unknown man, who remained in the darkest corner of the saloon. The other young man vainly tried to get a response from the veteran outlaw.

'We're here just like you wanted,' he said eagerly.

Black remained silent for some moments. Then he straightened up and slowly turned around until his back rested against the damp wooden counter. He stared like an eagle across the smoke-filled saloon at the man sitting behind a green baize card table. Something was wrong and it did not take Black long to figure out what it was. The man was neither drinking nor smoking. He was simply eyeing Black.

'You angry with us, Brad?' the shorter of the young outlaws asked Black.

'Shut the hell up,' Black ordered. He stepped away from the bar and pulled his gloves tight until you could see the outline of his knuckles through the leather.

Black continued to watch the seated man with unblinking eyes. Finally the sweat-sodden outlaw shouted out at the distant figure.

'I got me a feeling that you're either a lawman or a filthy bounty hunter, mister,' Black yelled across the saloon. His hands hovered over his gun grips. 'Which is it?'

The man stood and pushed the card table aside. He stepped forward until the morning sun caught the tin star pinned to his vest. The star glinted in the brilliant rays of sunlight that beamed through the saloon window.

The man pushed the tails of his coat over his gun grips and stared at the venomous Black.

'My names Baker,' the lawman said. His fingers flexed over his holstered guns. 'Sheriff Baker from Cordite County. I intend taking you back to stand trial, Black.'

'Is that one of your boys that's bin trailing me across the desert, Sheriff?' Black asked.

'If someone's bin trailing you he ain't belonging to me,' Baker snapped back.

Black lowered his head and studied the lawman. Baker was a big man, well over six foot tall and wider than most, but that suited the deadly Black. He liked large targets. They were harder to miss.

'How'd you know I'd be here, Sheriff?' he asked.

Sheriff Baker smiled. 'I didn't. The telegraph operator told me that them two young guns behind you received a message from you to meet them here. So I trailed them.'

Black smiled more broadly than the sheriff. 'You rode eighteen miles just to die? Hardly seems worth it.'

'Your Wanted poster says "dead or alive", Black,' Sheriff Baker drawled. 'Unbuckle your gunbelt and I'll see you get a fair trial.'

'That's mighty big of you, Sheriff,' Black growled. 'Trouble is I don't hanker after standing trial. Folks get themselves strung up that way.'

The sheriff took another step.

It was a mistake. As his boot leather pushed the sawdust aside Black drew both his guns and blasted them in quick succession. The entire building shook as the deafening noise of the six-shooters rocked its wooden fabric.

A look of total surprise, horror and pain spread across Sheriff Baker's face as the bullets ripped through his chest and exploded out of his back. For a brief moment the lawman just stared in disbelief at the man he had intended to arrest. Black mercilessly cocked his hammers again and fired.

The second volley punched the lawman off his feet. Baker twisted on his heels, then crashed to the floor. A crimson spray of blood hung in the air before falling like rain. His lifeless eyes remained open as Bradley Black walked across the saloon and shook his spent casings over his body.

Black said nothing as he pulled fresh bullets from his belt and slid them into his smoking weapons. He then turned and walked back to the bar counter. Open-mouthed, the two young guns watched him. Black eyed both youngsters.

'Glad you showed up, boys,' he said, holstering his smoking guns. 'I got me a big job lined up and I need extra guns to back up my play.'

'You sent for us to back your play?' one of them gasped.

'Anyone as fast as you are d-don't need anyone to b-back up his play, Brad,' the other one stammered.

Black downed his whiskey and looked at each of them in turn.

'I've got me a high-paying job in San Miguel,' Black told them. 'I need a couple of boys in case someone tries to back-shoot me. You interested?'

They both nodded.

Black moved around them, glanced at his bloody handiwork and started back for the swing doors. The two outlaws ran after him into the blazing sunshine. They watched him mount his grey, then hurried to their own horses.

'Who hired you, Brad?'

'The General,' Black replied.

'I never heard of him.'

'Me neither.'

'That don't matter none. You just do as I tell you or I'll kill you like I killed that starpacker,' Black growled. He pulled his reins free and turned the grey. 'Understand?'

'We understand, Brad,' the younger outlaw said.

Black rose in his stirrups and stared out at the rider who was still following him. He took a deep breath, then tapped his spurs and rode round the corner of the saloon. The two horsemen followed him closely.

Black pointed at a violent sandstorm which was raging ahead of them, and turned to the young men. The sight of his hardened features chilled them both to the bone.

'We're headed that way,' he said.

'Into that storm?'

Black cast a cruel smile upon the young outlaws and nodded knowingly.

'Yep. Right into that storm. Any objections?'

There were no objections. The three riders spurred and drove their mounts across the arid terrain at breakneck pace and towards the raging storm.

More than thirty minutes had passed since the trio of outlaws had left the dead lawman lying in a pool of his own gore. The acrid smell of gunsmoke had not had time to drift from the saloon as the lone horseman rode into the scattering of buildings and passed close to where Sheriff Baker still lay upon the blood-soaked sawdust.

Scattergun Smith had heard the gunplay. He paused his mustang beside the boardwalk and looked down upon the pale-faced bartender.

'I'm trailing a scum-sucking *hombre* named Black,' Scattergun said. 'You seen him?'

'I sure have. He just killed a starpacker inside my place,' the bartender replied in a rush of words. 'Killed him like he was swatting a fly.'

'That sounds like Black,' the rider said. 'Which way did he go?'

The shaking man pointed at the sandstorm. 'He went thataway. I heard him mention San Miguel.'

'Black's headed straight into a sandstorm,' Scattergun said. 'I reckon he knows that I'm gaining on him. He figures that storm will shake me off, but he's wrong.'

The storm was in total contrast to the rest of the devilish terrain. It was darkness and turmoil, while the desert was scorched by the relentless sun. Scattergun did not like storms at the best of times but he knew that he would have to follow his prey wherever he went.

'How come you're hunting that *hombre*, stranger?' the bartender asked, mopping his brow with a handkerchief. 'He ain't the sort of critter I'd like to catch up with.'

'I ain't that all-fired wishful to catch him, barkeep,' Scattergun said. He gathered up his loose leathers.

'Then why are you chasin' him?'

'I intend killing him, friend.' Scattergun touched the brim of his hat. Spurring his horse, he turned away to continue trailing Bradley Black across the arid desert.

The bartender watched as Scattergun rode his lathered-up mustang towards the sandstorm. He was still watching when the determined horseman disappeared from view, engulfed by the swirling clouds of dust.

TWO

The sandstorm had hardly slowed the pace of the three riders as they navigated a course through its blinding grit towards the distant border town. Black led the way, his two newly acquired followers trailing the tail of his grey through the blinding sand like hounds pursuing a wily fox.

Eventually the three sweat-sodden riders broke free of the merciless sandstorm and thundered away from the chaos that had encompassed them. The oppressive sun seemed to hang motionless in the heavens above the outlaws as they drove their mounts on towards the wind-scorched town ahead of them.

Bradley Black led his greenhorn cohorts towards the town. He balanced in his stirrups, hovering over the mane of his grey as Keno Mason and

Dade Coleman followed. He glanced back at the cloud of dark ferocity behind them and knew that, although it was merely an annoying sandstorm at present, it was growing with every beat of his blackened heart.

He knew that in this territory weather could change quickly. Sandstorms developed into far more dangerous phenomena. He had seen entire towns flattened by unholy twisting winds of Biblical proportions. Towns could be reduced to matchwood in the blink of an eye.

Black drove his grey on.

'I see a livery at the far end of the town, boys,' he yelled. 'We'll leave the nags there.'

Mason and Coleman whipped their mounts in pursuit of Black. Just like the man they followed, they wanted to put as much distance as they could between themselves and the storm.

Black gritted his teeth and narrowed his eyes as his exhausted mount continued to obey the spurs of its master. The grey had been unable to stretch its long legs and gallop until the three riders had broken free of the choking sandstorm. Now it was different and each of the ruthless horsemen was able to allow his mount to forge a route toward the distant San Miguel.

The sun beat down and warmed their bones as they spurred on. Although none of them would dare say anything, they were thankful that at last they had reached San Miguel.

Black eased back on his reins as he surveyed the small settlement carefully. He watched the wires on the telegraph poles swaying as the storm gusted across the lifeless sand.

The veteran outlaw looked at his two followers, then pointed at the wires.

'Shoot them wires,' he ordered. 'We don't want anybody getting the law down here.'

Mason and Coleman obediently drew their six-shooters and fanned their hammers. A half-dozen shots echoed throughout San Miguel. The wires were severed.

The three horsemen moved into the town. They each knew that the deafening volley of shots had cleared its streets.

Black squinted at the storm as the wind rotated the massive wall of sand with a destructive force capable of ripping the flesh from the bones of the unwary. He and his trail-weary men had thought that somehow they had survived the worst of it, but now it looked as though the worst was yet to come.

Black turned and faced San Miguel. When he

was rested up he would seek out the mysterious man known as the General. Then he would discover what he had to do to earn the small fortune he had been promised.

The storm would not strike for at least a few hours, the devilish outlaw told himself. Time enough to rest up before he set out to find the General.

As he led the way into the small town, Black recalled the stranger who had been dogging his trail.

Who was he?

Sheriff Baker had not known.

Black thrust his spurs into the flanks of the grey. The horse obeyed its master and, somehow finding a new pace, it thundered into the heart of San Miguel.

As they slowed to a trot Black wiped the dust from his grimy features and eased his reins back. The horses stopped beside a trough and started to quench their thirst.

Black looked at the sandstorm as his men dismounted. Again he thought about the man who had been trailing him, and he spat at the ground.

Whoever he was he was a dead man, Black vowed silently.

He looped his leg over his bedroll, dropped to the ground and rested his temple against the saddle.

'What's troubling you, Brad.' Mason asked. 'We're here now.'

Black pushed himself away from the horse. 'I know. The trouble is there was some varmint trailing me back yonder.'

'Who was trailing you?' Coleman wondered.

'I'm not sure,' Black answered, 'but I reckon we'll find out soon enough.'

'When we going to see the General, Brad?' Coleman asked nervously.

Black spat. 'I'll be going alone. You and Keno will remain in town and wait until I've sealed the deal.'

'What kinda job do you figure this General wants you for?'

Black raised an eyebrow. 'I reckon it must involve killing, Dade. Nobody sends for Bradley Black unless they want someone killed.'

THREE

The Long Branch was full to overflowing as Black and his two cohorts entered the saloon. For a moment none of the customers or bargirls noticed the three new faces who had entered the busy saloon. Soon that would change.

The tinny piano rang out as Black, Mason and Coleman stood before the swinging doors. They eyed the room with a mixture of contempt and eagerness.

They moved through the crowd towards the bar. Black used the barrels of his .45s like machetes. Men of every possible shape and size fell as he hacked a course towards the long counter with Mason and Coleman at his spurred heels.

The bartender suddenly saw the three outlaws forcing their way to him. He swallowed hard and leaned to one side. The sight of his customers stretched out in the outlaws' wake horrified the trembling man.

'Whiskey,' Black demanded. His thumbs hauled back on the hammers of his .45s, which were now aimed over the counter. 'Three bottles.'

The bartender turned and grabbed three dusty bottles from a shelf. He placed them down before Mason and Coleman, then swallowed hard and backed away.

'Tell me. Has this town got itself a funeral parlour, barkeep?' Black asked. He twirled his guns on his fingers and glared straight into the eyes of the shaking bartender.

The man nodded.

A cruel smile stretched across the hardened features of the deadly outlaw. Black signalled to his men. They turned and walked back through the groups of stunned and uncomprehending saloon patrons, towards the swing doors.

Black aimed his gun at the bartender's crotch. 'Just remember that, boy. You'd hate to go visiting the undertaker at your tender age.'

Every eye watched the outlaws as they left the

saloon. Not a word was uttered by the startled customers. The only sound to be heard inside the Long Branch was the mocking creaks of the batwings as they swung on their unoiled hinges.

It was more than an hour later when Scattergun Smith rode up a ridge and steadied his weary mount before spurring it on. He was of a breed that was unable to quit hunting its chosen prey. Whatever obstacles were placed in his path, Scattergun just continued to trail the outlaw through the vicious sandstorm and refused to stop. It was said that nothing could ever deter him once he had the scent in his nostrils.

It was as though there were an invisible rope joining both hunter and hunted. Nothing could sever that invisible bond, apart from death.

Braced against the elements, Scattergun rode on.

The deeper that Scattergun rode into the blinding tempest the worse it became. It hit the lone rider from all sides as he fought to control his spooked horse. It had grown far more brutal than it had been when Black and his men had journeyed through it.

Now it was relentlessly buffeting both horse and

rider and hampering his attempt to escape its torment. Although he had no tracks to follow his honed instincts told him which way to go. Yet it was no easy task trailing anyone blind. Somehow Scattergun managed to remain in his saddle and keep his valiant mount upright as the wild wind vainly tried to unsettle them both.

Desperately he drove his bloodstained spurs into the flanks of his all but exhausted mount and forged a straight and true trail towards the small border town. The intrepid horseman did not appear either to notice or care how cruel the relentless storm became. All he could think about was catching up with Black and killing him.

Scattergun had a fire burning in his innards that could only be extinguished when he had made the infamous Black pay for his misdeeds.

Soon he would reach San Miguel, find Black and administer his own brand of justice. That single thought was enough to continue driving Scattergun onwards in pursuit of the elusive outlaw.

If anyone could have seen through the impenetrable dust they would have observed a strange sight sitting astride the obedient mustang. For the rider had draped his bedroll blanket over his shoulders as a shield against the skin-tearing sand that rode on the wings of the savage wind.

His head was hidden beneath a makeshift cover made from an old feed sack with two crude holes cut into its woven hemp fabric. The drawstring of his battered Stetson held the sack in place as he continued to jab his spurs and force the weary mustang on towards San Miguel.

Scattergun Smith was a man whom everyone claimed to know but few actually did. The only thing certain about him was that he was a loner.

Even his name bore no relation to his true identity. It was simply a handle which had been branded on to him when he had first entered the realms of legend.

Whoever Scattergun really was, he was a man driven by vengeance. Yet that desire for vengeance was aimed at only one man. The accursed creature known as Bradley Black. Scattergun Smith had never revealed his reason for wanting Black dead.

All Scattergun would ever say was that it was personal.

Perhaps it was because Black had no morality in his entire body. It was well known that he earned his blood money from his ability with his guns.

In Scattergun's book, men who killed were bad

33

enough. Men who killed for money were even worse.

Maybe nobody would ever discover where Scattergun's origins lay. It was as though he had simply appeared one day and from then on had just existed. From that day forth Scattergun Smith had become an almost mythical creature whom few would ever truly understand.

The gaunt horseman drove his bloody spurs into the flesh of his exhausted mount as he sensed he was nearing San Miguel. The faithful animal beneath his saddle obeyed its master's urging and kept up its laboured pace.

Like something from the most horrific of nightmares, Scattergun Smith emerged from the sandstorm at the very boundary of the small town and drew rein. To any onlookers, the sight of the horseman could not have been more fearful.

Both horse and rider were caked in dust.

The mustang walked on towards the wooden marker at the very edge of town. Scattergun eased back on his reins to read the few words scrawled upon its weathered surface.

'San Miguel. Population four hundred and twenty,' he drawled as his long fingers stroked the rows of shotgun shells that hung across his chest in crossed belts. 'Not for long.'

Menacing laughter came from beneath the hemp mask as his icy stare focused upon the town that lay before him. A mixture of brick and wooden buildings lay ahead of him, intermingled with a few smaller whitewashed adobes.

Scattergun Smith gathered the ends of his long leathers in his hands and surveyed the town carefully. Water glinted in horse troughs as the rays of the bright sunlight danced across their tempting surfaces like diamond necklaces.

The flared nostrils of the fearful mustang could smell the precious liquid but did not dare move a muscle towards the troughs until its master commanded it do so.

Scattergun spurred the weary animal and began the final leg of his journey into the little town.

San Miguel was silent. Its streets were empty. The strange horseman knew that his sudden appearance had been observed and news of the arrival of something resembling a creature from the depths of nightmares had spread through San Miguel faster than a brush fire.

They had seen him.

The intrepid rider did not care who witnessed his arrival unless it was the outlaw he sought. But as the sand-caked horse set one weary hoof in front of another through the streets of San Miguel its master could not see any sign of the man he hunted. Wherever Black was he was not in plain view.

The horse had the scent of water in its nostrils but its master could smell whiskey. He steered the mustang towards the nearest saloon. As they approached the unpainted wooden building his eyes never rested. Behind the two holes in the feed sack his gaze darted from left to right, vainly seeking the lethal outlaw.

A thought occurred to Scattergun.

There were meant to be 420 souls living in this sunbaked town, yet so far he had not seen even a hint of life apart from a few saddle horses tied to various hitching-rails along the wide street.

None of them was a grey gelding like the one he knew Bradley Black rode.

He diverted his attention to the saloon.

There were those who might have likened his progress to the arrival of the grim reaper as Scattergun Smith closed the distance between himself and the drinking hole.

FOUR

The ominous figure pointed his mustang towards the front of the saloon. Then Scattergun Smith steered his travel-stained horse along the street to the sparkling water trough. They had seen him, he thought. Dozens of eyes in hidden faces had spotted his arrival as soon as he had entered the small town.

The sandstorm continued to grow in intensity on the edge of town. Apart from its howling there was no other noise.

Scattergun realized the townsfolk had probably never witnessed anyone quite so hideous as himself before. He allowed his weary mount to find its own pace and dropped the blanket from his shoulders. It fell on to the saddle cantle.

As he neared the saloon his high vantage point allowed him to see over its swing doors and into the saloon. Eyes in the faces of startled and frightened people watched his approach.

It was uncertain upon which side of the unmarked border San Miguel lay. Perhaps that was why there seemed to be no law here, he mused. Since entering San Miguel Scattergun had seen no sign of a sheriff's office anywhere along the wide thoroughfare.

There was nothing unusual about that in these parts, for it was tough getting anyone to pin a tin star on his vest when the territory was full of folks who tended to use such decorations for target practice.

The solidly built wood and brick saloon stood proudly in what Scattergun assumed was the main street. It rubbed shoulders with a barbershop and a number of other stores. However, it was only the saloon that drew the horseman's attention.

Scattergun guided his mount to a hitching pole outside the large saloon. He drew rein and then leaned back against his cantle and read the welcoming sign nailed firmly to the balcony railings. He brushed the sand off his sleeves and kept watching the people gathered within the saloon as they stared in disbelief at the terrifying sight of the man who had stopped his horse directly facing its swing doors.

'The Long Branch,' Smith read before removing his battered hat and the feed sack which had protected him from the sandstorm's fury.

He threw a long leg over his saddle-bags and slowly dismounted. With every action he could feel the eyes of the townsfolk gathered in the saloon, who he knew were watching him. He pushed the sack into the depths of his trail-coat pocket.

Scattergun Smith carefully secured his reins to the hitching pole near the full trough. His eyes darted from one awestruck face to another, as though daring anyone with the guts to step out and move towards him.

No one did. They simply watched.

The tall man cranked a cast-iron pump enough times for crystal-clear water to start flowing from its spout into the crude wooden trough. The mustang moved forward nervously and lowered its head to drink.

Scattergun pushed the tails of his long black coat over the pair of shotguns resting upon his hips. He then placed his Stetson over his dark hair and stepped up on to the saloon boardwalk.

He reached out with one of his long arms, pushed the swing doors inward and strode into the bar-room. He halted two steps in and waited for the batwings to stop swinging on their hinges before he advanced.

Even without his mask he looked no less dangerous. He walked across the sawdust-covered floor towards the bar counter slowly and with purpose. The saloon could have been in any of countless other Western towns. There was a familiarity about it that drew the long-legged man across its sawdust-covered floor to where a nervous bartender awaited his arrival.

The saloon's atmosphere was exactly like that of all of the other drinking holes he had ventured into over the years.

The potent aroma filled his flared nostrils. It was the combined stench of spilled liquor, cheap perfume and lingering tobacco smoke. Yet there was another scent that overwhelmed them all. It was the unmistakable smell of freshly spilled blood. Scattergun recognized it only too well.

His gaze darted around the saloon, then he looked down to the floor. Even freshly strewn sawdust could not disguise it from his flared nostrils. Blood had been spilled recently. An awful lot of blood.

Scattergun looked up at the frightened faces of the men and women on both sides of the bar counter. He touched the brim of his hat at them, then rested a boot upon the brass rail that ran the length of the counter behind unemptied spittoons.

His cold eyes focused on the thin bartender.

'You got any whiskey in this saloon?' Scattergun asked. He pulled a long slim cigar from his breast pocket and placed it between his teeth.

The bartender nodded nervously; sweat trickled down his face.

'We surely have, stranger,' he stammered.

Scattergun placed a golden half-eagle down and slid it across the surface of the counter. It made a ripple in the spilled liquor.

'Then bring me a bottle, *amigo*,' he instructed. 'The best you got.'

The thin barman turned and walked to where dust-covered bottles stood just beneath a grimy mirror. Scattergun silently watched as the bartender brushed the dust from the bottles until his shaking hands lit upon the one he was searching for.

'Will this'un do?' the man asked, holding the

bottle at arm's length. 'It's the best we got.'

'It'll do just fine.' The tall stranger gave a nod of his head and then curled his finger at the bartender. The saloon worker advanced towards his latest customer with the bottle gripped in his shaking hands. Scattergun glanced at the sealed bottle, then gazed into the barman's eyes.

'What you want?' the bartender asked.

'I'm wondering who got themselves pistol-whipped in here, friend?' Scattergun scratched a match and cupped its flame to the tip of his cigar. He sucked in smoke and watched as the nervous bartender placed the whiskey bottle down in front of him. The bartender then snatched a thimble glass from a small pyramid and placed it beside the dusty bottle.

'I don't understand,' he said nervously.

Scattergun raised his eyebrows. 'I figure you do.'

The barman moved to his cash drawer and pulled it open. He collected the change before dropping the golden coin into it. He closed the drawer and turned to face the tall stranger who now stood beneath a cloud of cigar smoke.

Scattergun held out his hand and accepted his change.

'Much obliged,' he drawled ominously.

The dozen or so people who had shied away from the counter when Scattergun had entered the Long Branch were now starting to move closer. Scattergun peeled the paper seal from around the neck of the bottle and crushed it in his hand. He dropped it casually into the mouth of a spittoon, then raised the bottle to his teeth.

As his teeth gripped the cork the nervous bartender cleared his throat and spoke.

'Are you in town on business?' he asked. He watched the stranger pull the cork from the neck of the bottle and fill his glass with a measure of its amber contents.

Scattergun stared straight at the inquisitive man. The other customers continued to edge closer to him. He spat the cork at the sawdust and raised the cigar back to his lips. He inhaled deeply as his eyes burned into the bartender's face. There was no hint of emotion in his expression as smoke drifted from between his teeth.

'Why'd you ask?' Scattergun hissed.

The bartender twitched. He regretted opening his mouth and it showed. More sweat ran down from his thinning hair and dripped on to his starched collar.

'No reason,' he answered, gulping. 'I was just

wondering if you was here on business. San Miguel ain't the kinda town folks come to unless they're lost.'

'I ain't lost,' the dust-covered stranger said.

The bartender mopped his brow with his sleeve. 'Are you here on business?'

'You might say so,' Scattergun answered, the hint of a knowing smile crossing his face. 'I do have business of sorts to settle in San Miguel.'

The bartender was getting as brave as the bar-girls and customers. He rested his wrists on the counter and watched as the dust-caked figure downed shots of whiskey in rapid succession. Yet no matter how many shots of whiskey he swallowed it did not seem to have any effect on him. The bartender tilted his head as he studied the stranger.

'We've never seen you before in these parts,' he remarked. 'You ain't bin here before, have you?'

Scattergun paused and sucked smoke into his lungs again as his piercing stare focused on the inquisitive bartender.

'Nope. I've never ridden this far south before.'

'I figured as much.' The bartender nodded and looked at the faces of his other patrons. 'What kinda business are you intending doing?'

'You'll find out soon enough,' Scattergun told him.

Just then the hinges of the swing doors behind Scattergun creaked as they were pushed open. Every living soul in the Long Branch saloon stared at the young man who entered. They watched his arrogant approach.

Only Scattergun Smith remained with his back to the youngster who strutted towards him. Scattergun watched the youth's reflection in the mirror behind the bartender. The bartender's face went ashen as his eyes fixed upon the latest visitor to his saloon.

Joey Bulmer was barely twenty and had a face that looked as though it had yet to start sprouting whiskers. Like so many young men he had yet to prove himself, but was determined to try. He had a solitary holstered gun strapped around his lean hips. The belt hung from his left hip so that the holstered gun grip was within easy reach of his right hand.

With his hand hovering over his weapon Bulmer kept on moving towards Scattergun's broad back. The young gun stopped two feet away from the bloody spurs of the stranger.

'Now we don't want no trouble, Joey,' the bartender told the young man, who seemed to be intent on proving his manhood.

'I ain't afeared of no critter that rides into town with a feed sack over his ugly face, Chuck,' Bulmer snorted fearlessly. 'Turn around, stranger. Turn around and face me or I'll shoot you dead. Are you the *hombre* that split a dozen heads earlier?'

Scattergun did not respond. He kept on filling his lungs with cigar smoke and his glass with whiskey.

The bartender seemed more anxious than his dusty customer.

'Now go on home, Joey,' he shouted. 'This ain't the gent that cracked your pa's head open.'

'I ain't going no place,' Bulmer snarled. 'I don't like strangers and I don't like this'un. He best get going before I teach him a lesson.'

Scattergun placed the glass over the open neck of his bottle and gripped the cigar in the corner of his mouth. Slowly he turned and faced the youngster, one eyebrow raised.

'You want something?' he asked the frowning Bulmer.

Bulmer swallowed hard. The sight of the stranger up close was something he had not anticipated. The youngster remained planted to the spot as his eyes darted over Scattergun's daunting appearance. The two holstered shotguns and the crossed belts of cartridges were unlike anything he had ever encountered before.

'You better get on that old nag of yours and ride,' Joey Bulmer managed to say, his hand going closer to the grip of his .45. 'I'll kill you if you don't.'

Scattergun blew smoke across the distance that separated them and smiled when Bulmer coughed. It was not a friendly smile but the sort of smile that can turn milk sour.

'I reckon you might try, sonny,' he said through the smoke that drifted from his mouth. 'Trouble is, I'd have to kill you and that ain't part of my plans.'

Bulmer was shaking but, with the stubbornness of youth, refused to back away from the tall stranger.

'Big talk for a saddle bum,' he snarled. 'You don't scare me none though. I'll kill you if you don't get out of town.'

Scattergun nodded. 'I reckon you might be just dumb enough to try.'

Before Joey Bulmer could utter another word, Scattergun grabbed the young gun by the neck and pulled him towards him violently. Scattergun twisted like a matador as Bulmer's head was dragged into the mahogany bar counter.

As the painful sound of a skull colliding with the bar counter's woodwork filled the Long Branch, Scattergun grabbed the back of the unconscious Bulmer's pants.

The bartender moved to one side to watch Scattergun hoist the limp Bulmer off the floor and toss him over the wet counter. The young pretender crashed to the floor at the bartender's feet.

'Reckon he'll be asleep for a while,' Scattergun opined, and sighed.

'You could be right,' the bartender agreed, and gulped.

As though nothing had happened Scattergun clapped his hands together and then resumed his drinking. He downed another glass of the whiskey and noticed the crowd getting even closer.

'I thought you was gonna have to shoot young Joey, stranger,' Chuck the bartender said.

'I don't waste shotgun shells on little boys trying to prove themselves, barkeep,' Scattergun replied. He tapped ash from his cigar and looked to either side at the men and women who were now uncomfortably close.

A bargirl moved so close to Scattergun that he tilted his head, looking down upon her and into the cleavage of her dress. He said nothing as his eyes surveyed her scarcely concealed form and his nostrils scented her stale perfume.

'I know who you are,' she said cheekily as her fingertips traced along the shotgun closer to her.

'Who am I?' he asked.

The patrons moved in even closer. They all stretched their necks in order to hear.

She placed her back against the wooden bar counter, rested her elbows on its sodden surface and played with the frilly trim of her dress as it tried to keep her ample bosom restrained.

'You're that critter they call Scattergun Smith, ain't you?' She smiled whilst her eyes drifted over him. 'I've heard tales about you.'

The bartender loosened his stiff collar with his index finger. He looked at the bargirl.

'Scattergun Smith?'

'That's who this is.' The female was well beyond her best days but there was still a fire smouldering in her. 'That's your name, ain't it?'

He nodded gently.

She looked confused. 'Ain't it your name?'

'Guess it is,' Scattergun sighed. 'Leastways, that's what folks call me.'

'I thought so.' She laughed loudly. 'You're a

mighty handsome critter under all that dust. My name's Millie.'

Scattergun held both bottle and glass in his grip and eyed Millie as another buxom bargirl floated around him like a fly around a garbage pail. Scattergun turned away from the bar and walked to a card table. His impressive spurs jangled out a mournful tune as he strode towards it. Scattergun set the bottle down on its torn baize, placed the glass beside it and then sat down.

His narrowed eyes scanned every living creature within the Long Branch. Its patrons, in varying degrees of sobriety, had followed him across the sawdust and were now hovering around the table and its chairs.

He pushed the brim of his Stetson back off his forehead and filled his glass again with the amber liquor. Scattergun noted that only Chuck the bartender had remained behind the wooden counter, with his foot on the crumpled youngster.

Scattergun raised an eyebrow and looked into each face in turn. Folk were watching his every move as he refilled his glass for the umpteenth time.

Scattergun downed another shot of whiskey and savoured its fumes as the two girls sat on hard-back chairs to either side of him, looking at the strangely adapted weapons that rested against his thighs. Millie stroked the shaft of the shotgun as though it were something else.

'You here to kill someone?' she asked boldly.

Scattergun nodded at her. 'Maybe I am. Why'd you ask?'

'She's plumb nosy,' the other bargirl said, and she eased herself closer. 'I'm not nosy. There are a lot of things I can do with my mouth other than gab. My name's Mary.'

He replaced the cigar between his teeth. He narrowed his eyes as he studied the females' attributes.

'Has either of you gals ever heard of an *hombre* known as Bradley Black?' he asked. Both bargirls straightened up on their seats, fear filling their painted faces.

'Bradley Black?' Mary repeated.

'Ain't that the critter who come in here earlier?' Millie asked her friend. 'That's what Chuck said his name was. Chuck reckons he's seen that critter's face on a circular.'

Scattergun noticed that every man in the saloon had turned when they heard the outlaw's name.

'He was in here?' Scattergun nodded.

51

The talkative bargirl pulled the straps of her dress up as though she no longer wanted to display her assets.

'He was in here earlier,' she whispered. 'Got three bottles of whiskey.'

'And. . . ?' Scattergun pressed.

Mary gestured to Millie that they had best not say any more. They stood and gyrated back to the counter just as the dazed figure of Joey Bulmer staggered from behind the bar counter and fled from the saloon with his tail tucked between his legs.

Scattergun laughed to himself and poured another glass of whiskey. He watched Bulmer push the swing doors apart and escape to the street. The doors had not stopped swinging as thoughts of the devilish Black returned to Scattergun.

Black had a talent for filling innocent folks like these with terror, he thought. It was an ability Scattergun vowed to put an end to.

Scattergun studied the buxom females as they retreated to the far end of the saloon like frightened children. He lowered his head and sighed.

'Reckon this well has run dry.'

Everyone inside the Long Branch watched as the stranger left the half-full whiskey bottle on the card table next to the thimble glass. Scattergun strode back towards the batwings.

He pushed the swing doors apart and walked out into the blazing sunshine. His eyes surveyed the main street. He noted three hotels of various sizes and concluded that Bradley Black could be holed up in any of them.

He rubbed his jaw, then tugged the long leathers free from the hitching pole.

The ominous sound of the approaching storm drew his attention as he stepped down upon the white sand. It was getting worse and getting closer.

FIVE

Sitting on the balcony of the highest building in San Miguel three gruesome figures were quietly making their way through the whiskey Black had acquired earlier, when Keno Mason glanced down from their high vantage point and focused on the figure leading his mount away from the Long Branch. Mason rubbed his filthy features across his sleeve and glanced at his cohorts.

'That *hombre* makes us look clean,' he said as Black watched the heavily armed stranger leading his horse towards the distant livery stable.

'So that's the bastard who's bin trailing me,' Black raged. 'I figured it had to be him.'

Coleman lowered his bottle from his lips. 'You know him?'

'I know him.' Black nodded. 'He's bin a thorn in my side for a real long time.'

Mason and Coleman watched Black as he brooded.

'Either of you know who that *hombre* is?' Black asked. He lifted the neck of his bottle to his lips and took a long swig.

Coleman moved away from the doorway to the room and looked over the wooden railing. He shook his head and turned back to the others.

'Nope, I ain't ever seen him before, Keno,' Coleman replied. 'Reckon he only just rode into town though, by the state of his horse.'

'Maybe he's a cowpoke?' Mason suggested.

'That ain't no cowpoke, boys,' Black said coldly.

'How can you tell?' Mason walked back into the shade of the hotel room. 'Cowboys come in all shapes and sizes, Brad.'

'That's true, but I've never seen a cowboy packing two double-barrelled shotguns in hand-tooled shooting rigs strapped to his hips, Keno,' Black growled. 'That *hombre* might be many things but he sure ain't a cowpoke.'

Both Coleman and Mason stared at the troubled Black, who continued to watch the stranger lead his exhausted mount towards the livery stable.

'He's toting shotguns on his hips, Brad?' Coleman asked.

'He sure is, Dade.' Black spat and turned on his heel. He walked across the balcony, straight into the room he had rented for himself and his cronies. 'And there's only one dude I know who favours shotguns like that.'

'Who would that be?' Mason asked. He watched the nervous older man pace around the room like a cornered mountain lion.

Black stopped and stared at his hirelings.

'Scattergun Smith,' he replied.

Keno Mason rose back to his feet and squinted out into the sunbaked street. Scattergun was now too far away from the hotel for even his young eyes to make him out clearly. He turned.

'You reckon that Scattergun has been trailing you all this time, Brad?' Mason asked. 'Why would he do that?'

'He's got his reasons.' Black lifted his whiskey bottle to his lips and vainly tried to quench his thirst with the fiery liquid. 'Me and him got us unfinished business.'

'Is he after the reward money on your head, Brad?' Mason piped up again. He rested his hips on the end of his cot.

Black shook his head. 'He don't hunt bounty.'

'Then why does he keep dogging you?' Dade Coleman asked. He bit the tip off a fat cigar and spat it out.

'Like I said, he got his reasons,' Black growled.

Keno Mason scratched his unshaven lower lip with his thumbnail thoughtfully.

'He can't be much of a shot if he favours shotguns, Brad,' he suggested.

Bradley Black shrugged.

'He likes buckshot. I never heard of anyone getting the better of him in a showdown, boy,' he growled. 'When Scattergun squeezes his triggers there ain't a whole lot left of what he is shooting at.'

Coleman gripped the cigar in his teeth and looked at the veteran outlaw.

'Why is Scattergun hell-bent on catching you, Brad?'

'He got a grievance with me, Dade.' Black snarled. 'A real bad grievance that he won't let up on until one of us is dead.'

'If he's toting two shotguns like you say, I'd not go up against him, Brad,' Mason said with a shrug. 'He needs killing but not head-on killing. Them guns of his could blow a damn big hole in anyone foolish enough to try from the front.'

'He's gotta be bushwhacked,' Black said firmly.

The others nodded in agreement.

Coleman cupped the flame of the match he had just ignited and raised it to his cigar. As blue smoke trailed over his head he edged closer with the same look of uncertainty on his face.

'He didn't look so fearsome to me,' he remarked. 'He looked real tuckered by the storm, though.'

The words had barely left his lips when Black, who had been staring at him sternly, grabbed Coleman's greasy shirt collar and pulled the man towards him.

'Are you serious, Dade?' the taller man growled. 'A mountain lion wouldn't look fearsome from up here, but it's still gonna rip the hide off you given half a chance. Don't underestimate that bastard. That's Scattergun Smith and he's as deadly as a sidewinder.'

Coleman nodded fearfully. 'I know he's dangerous, Brad. I was just saying that he didn't look so dangerous the way he was leading that mustang up the street. He's plumb tuckered.'

Black released his grip.

'Scattergun is plumb dangerous even when he's

asleep, Dade,' he snarled forcefully. 'He don't take prisoners. That *hombre* is meaner than hell.'

'And he's after your hide,' Mason added.

'And he's after my hide,' Black agreed with the youngest of their small band.

Black pulled both his guns from their holsters and, as was his habit, checked that they were in full working order. As his anxious fingers rotated their chambers he glared at Mason.

'I never figured on him,' he snorted. 'Scattergun could spoil the job the General wants me to do. We could lose us a small fortune unless we get rid of him.'

The youngest outlaw nodded.

'You're right,' he agreed. 'We just gotta get rid of Scattergun.'

'The storm that's coming might help us achieve that a damn sight easier than facing him in the full glare of that hellish sun, boys,' Black suggested.

Coleman looked out of the window and grinned. 'That storm is looking real mean. I reckon you're right. It might help us bushwhack the famous Scattergun Smith, now you mention it, Brad.'

Black was thoughtful. He walked across the room and sat on his cot.

'That storm will cover our backs if it keeps on growing,' he said. 'Even Scattergun can't try to kill me with his eyes full of sand.'

Keno Mason nodded. 'What if he registers here and sees our names on the ledger?'

Black shook his head. 'I just made a mark and he don't know either of you boys. Besides, I told the clerk that if anyone asks questions it might be a fatal mistake if he answers them.'

They all laughed.

Black rose to his feet. He rammed his six-shooters into their holsters and stepped back out on to the balcony. He could still see the mysterious figure leading his mustang towards the towering livery stable.

'I don't think that critter knows what a soft bed feels like, boys,' he said. 'I bet he don't ever sleep like normal folks. We're safe here.'

'When are you gonna head on out to see the General, Brad?' Coleman wondered. 'Scattergun being here has made it kinda tricky, ain't it?'

'I'll head on out when the storm hits town,' Black answered firmly. 'The sand will give me all the cover I need.'

Coleman moved to Black's side and muttered through cigar smoke.

'Smart thinking.'

Black nodded. 'I know. And the storm ought to give you boys enough cover to get the drop on his stinking hide. He don't know either of you.'

Mason rose to his feet and marched to both his troubled cohorts.

'It'll be a turkey shoot, Brad.' He chuckled.

Black gave a nod. 'Between the two of you Scattergun don't stand a chance, Keno.'

The youngest outlaw grinned. 'I'm sure gonna enjoy snuffing out his damn candle, Brad.'

All three laughed. The youngest of the group got to his feet and sniffed the air. He then sniffed his clothing and those of his cohorts.

'We're stinking, Brad,' he said, pointing at his trail-worn gear. 'We need us a bath and new duds. We smell worse than our horses.'

Black gave a firm nod.

'You're right,' he drawled. 'We do stink.'

'I don't want to take no damn bath, Brad,' Coleman grumbled. 'We ain't here to pretty ourselves up, no matter how bad we need a bath.'

'Cleaning ourselves up will kill some time and allow our horses to rest up in the stables, Dade.' Mason smiled. 'Quit worrying.'

Black swung on his heel and glared at the

younger outlaws.

'It'll kill some time before the storm reaches this town, boys,' he said. 'After we've killed some time we can kill Scattergun as well.'

Black rested a hand on Mason's shoulder.

'Going up agin Scattergun is risky, Keno,' he warned.

Mason grinned. 'You sent for me and Dade to earn ourselves a big pay-day, Brad. We can't do the job on our lonesome, without you, so we gotta kill Scattergun.'

'Keno's right,' Coleman agreed. 'There just ain't no other way. We'll kill Scattergun before he kills you.'

Black ran a hand across his neck and reluctantly nodded as he moved back to the balcony and gazed out into the sun-drenched street and then further out at the storm, which was getting closer.

'All you gotta remember is that Scattergun is mighty dangerous, boys.' He sighed. 'Kill him any way you can and, whatever you do, don't let him draw them shotguns.'

'Can I have me a bath first, Brad?' Mason asked as he sucked on the neck of his bottle.

Black nodded and tossed silver dollars at his pal.

'Sure you can, Keno.' He smiled. 'Order three

tubs to be brung up here. We'll all have us a bath and put on fresh duds before we kill Scattergun.'

Mason got to his feet and headed for the door. He grabbed the handle, opened the door and left the room. Black turned to Coleman and lifted his whiskey bottle to his lips.

'Keno's right. We smell so bad that Scattergun might figure he's being cornered by a herd of skunks if we don't clean ourselves up first,' Black commented.

'The storm's getting closer,' Coleman said. He blew the ash from his cigar.

'Good.' Black nodded. 'I want that storm to be as thick as beef stew. I want it so bad out there that Scattergun won't even know what's hit him.'

Dade Coleman levelled his eyes at Black.

'What do you reckon the General wants you to do for him, Brad?' he asked.

'Killing, Dade,' Black replied bluntly. 'The General don't spend hard cash for nothing less than killing.'

SIX

The four heavily armed guards rode beside the private carriage as the coachman whipped his matched pair of palominos and kept them moving across the desolate landscape at pace. Concealed inside the luxurious coach and surrounded by such trimmings as only the wealthy could ever aspire to, Judge Cleveland Johnson sat staring through the glass panes of the carriage doors. He gripped a slender cigar between his store-bought teeth. He was the master of all he surveyed, for he had over 200 miners keeping him in the lap of luxury. Low wages and merciless guards ensured that Johnson remained far richer than most mortals could ever imagine possible.

Johnson had somehow elevated himself to the

position of judge ten years earlier. No one had ever questioned his right to the title. Wealthy men seldom have to prove anything, let alone what they call themselves.

Since first discovering gold a decade earlier, Johnson had slowly moved in ever grander circles. There were many who considered that his fortune would eventually take him to the very pinnacle of power. Johnson had no objections to being worshipped like a god, for that was exactly how he thought of himself. Gods were answerable to no one. He made his own rules and laws and knew that he had the firepower to back him up. Johnson had vowed never to allow anyone to take him back to his humble origins.

Anyone who even dared to make the attempt was quickly disposed of. The desert through which his magnificent coach was travelling was filled with the bodies of those who had tried.

The money he had earned from exploiting the precious ore had made him one of the most powerful and influential characters in the region. It had enabled him to buy almost anything he desired, including the title of judge.

Even with no practical knowledge of the law, Johnson still had the power of life and death in this remote land. His word was law in the gold-rich terrain that surrounded San Miguel.

The black carriage came in from the east and slowed as its driver steered the vehicle into the private stables that flanked a modest wooden building on the very edge of San Miguel.

This was just one of five homes belonging to Judge Cleveland Johnson. It was Johnson's habit to pay a monthly visit to each of the towns dotted around his goldmines. Known throughout the region as the 'killing judge', Johnson revelled in his power over his workforce and enjoyed dishing out his own brand of justice wherever he thought it was deserved.

His guards dismounted to stand beside the vehicle as the coachman climbed down and opened one of its doors. Johnson stepped out and dusted down his fine tailored suit. His eyes glanced around at his henchmen.

Just as he was about to enter the building by a side door his guards all drew their six-shooters at exactly the same moment. They aimed out from the shadows at the figure of Joey Bulmer as the youngster staggered through the sandstorm towards them.

The sound of hammers being cocked filled the

private stables as the four guards trained their weaponry on the bruised and battered Bulmer.

'Hold it right there, boy,' ordered Sam Dexter, the gruffest of the guards. 'What you want here?'

Bulmer stopped and rubbed his sore head. The lump on the top of his skull was as big as an egg.

'I got me some news for Judge Johnson,' he replied.

His curiosity aroused, Johnson pushed his way through the line of guards and looked long and hard at Bulmer.

'What kinda news, boy?' he asked.

'There's a gunman in town, Judge,' Bulmer told him. 'I tangled with him and got my head stove in. Someone said that he's a hired killer.'

Johnson curled his finger at Bulmer. The kid walked forward.

'A hired killer?' the judge repeated. 'Are you sure?'

Bulmer nodded. 'I'm dead sure, Judge. They say his name's Scattergun Smith. I tried to run him out of town but he was too fast for me.'

Dexter and the three other guards standing behind Johnson chuckled.

The laughter stopped instantly as Johnson raised his hand.

'What did you say his name was again?' the judge asked.

'Scattergun Smith, Judge,' Bulmer replied. 'He got himself a couple of sawn-down shotguns in fancy holsters. That critter is looking for blood.'

Johnson pulled a silver dollar from his jacket and handed it to Bulmer. 'Here. Tell me one more thing, boy. Where is this Scattergun Smith right now?'

Bulmer looked at the oncoming storm. He shrugged, then looked at the judge.

'He was in the Long Branch,' he said.

Johnson watched as the youngster ran back into the dust, then turned to face his guards. He looked troubled.

'What's wrong, Judge?' one of his guards named Festus Pike asked. 'What if he is a hired killer? It don't mean that he's bin hired to kill you.'

The expression on the self-proclaimed judge's face stiffened as he pondered on the news he had just heard. He tilted his head and pointed at two of his guards.

'Find this Scattergun Smith *hombre* and kill him,' Johnson ordered. 'Nobody locks horns with Cleveland Johnson.'

*

The trail-weary figure glanced over his shoulder as he led the exhausted mustang into the livery stable. He had noticed that the streets were still as empty as when he had first arrived in San Miguel. The only living souls he had seen were those inside the Long Branch saloon, and they, after he had muttered the name of Bradley Black, had turned from him as though he had leprosy.

Scattergun stopped in the middle of the livery and stood as still as a statue. His piercing eyes surveyed the interior of the building until every detail of the stable was branded into his memory.

There were a dozen horses in stalls and room for another five or six in the far corner. A sturdy wooden ladder rose twelve feet up to a hayloft. Shafts of sunlight gleamed into the building from a score of gaps in its walls' cladding and from an open window directly above the wide double doors. A large blacksmith's forge glowed eerily in the far corner. The only thing the livery stable lacked was any sign of the man who was meant to run the business.

Scattergun dropped his reins on the floor and walked to the forge. The heat from the coals warmed him as he looked about for someone to whom he could entrust his exhausted mount.

Apart from the stalled horses the place appeared to be deserted, but Scattergun had learned long ago that appearances could be deceptive.

Every sinew in his lean frame warned him that he was not alone. It was as if he could feel someone watching his every movement. Someone was observing him from the cover that shadows could only too easily provide.

He pushed his coat tails over his weapons and pulled a twisted cigar from between the ammunition belts that crossed his chest.

Scattergun placed the long slim cigar between his teeth and turned full circle as he vainly searched for even a hint of where the blacksmith might be secreted.

He picked up a poker which had been resting in the glowing coals. Scattergun lifted it with a gloved hand and touched the tip of his cigar.

Smoke filled his lungs.

Scattergun Smith tossed the poker on to the bed of coals and moved back to his mount. He had become aware of the spine-chilling sound of the sandstorm. The whole of the building creaked.

He glanced through the open doors.

His eyes focused upon the approaching storm. A

storm which he had survived but yet it dogged his trail. It was coming towards San Miguel as surely as night follows day. Scattergun blew a line of smoke at the ground and wondered how long it would be before the entire town would be engulfed.

Suddenly another sound interrupted his thoughts.

Faster than the blink of an eye, Scattergun drew one of his hefty weapons from his hand-crafted holsters. He cocked both its hammers as a huge man emerged from the shadows.

The impressive figure did not seem to be intimidated by the shotgun.

For a moment Scattergun had been ready to dish out death.

Then he relaxed as he watched the large bulky figure stride towards him. There was no mistaking a blacksmith. His muscular frame glistened in the shafts of sunlight that invaded the building.

'You intending on using that damn shotgun, mister?' the blacksmith asked. Reaching the forge he placed a blackened coffee pot upon its coals. 'If you ain't I'd be obliged if you'd put it away.'

Scattergun holstered the mighty weapon.

'I want to stable my horse for a couple of nights,' he told the blacksmith. 'He's plumb tuckered and needs grain and a rub down.'

The large man walked from the forge and inspected the animal. He returned his attention to its master. He looked Scattergun up and down and then spat at the ground.

'You've not treated this mustang kindly, stranger,' he said angrily. He turned his eyes again to the bleeding cuts on the animal's flanks.

'Reckon you don't value this pitiful critter as much as you ought.'

Scattergun lowered his head and glared at the blacksmith.

'You scolding me, friend?' he asked.

'Reckon so.' The blacksmith picked up the reins and led the mustang towards an empty stall. Scattergun followed.

'I happen to own that nag,' Scattergun said, smoke drifting from his lips. 'I still got the bill of sale in my saddle-bags if you'd care to look.'

The blacksmith raised the fender and hooked the stirrup on to the saddle horn.

'Just coz you paid for this mustang it don't give you the right to hurt the damn critter,' the big man said. 'You ripped its flesh to ribbons with them fancy spurs. That riles me.'

Scattergun walked around both the man and his

horse. He said nothing as his saddle was hauled off the horse's back and placed on a rail.

'You ought to be ashamed,' the blacksmith went on. He started to brush the horse down. 'Why'd you harm this horse? Don't you know how valuable a faithful horse is in these parts?'

'You wouldn't happen to be the town preacher, would you?' Scattergun growled. 'This ain't no church and you ain't got no pulpit.'

The muscular man paused for a moment, stared at Scattergun and then continued to brush the horse down.

'I just don't like seeing horses hurt,' he growled again. 'Makes me want to snap folks in half.'

Scattergun looked at the big blacksmith warily. His rippling muscles gleamed as sweat ran down from his hairy shoulders. He looked more than capable of making good on his warnings.

'I only spurred that critter 'coz we were stuck in that damn sandstorm and it was getting kind of dangerous,' Scattergun explained. 'He was tuckered and I had to try and get him woke up.'

The explanation did not impress the blacksmith.

'So you cut him up 'coz you were scared?' he asked.

Scattergun looked back through the large barn doors at the storm which was still raging as it slowly headed for San Miguel.

'I weren't scared, friend,' he said. 'I was terrified.'

The blacksmith placed a bucket of water in front of the mustang and watched as it drank. His bushy eyebrows rose. He marched to a feed sack and picked up a metal scoop. He filled the scoop with oats and then returned to the horse.

Scattergun watched as the gentle giant poured out the feed for the weary animal. He pulled the cigar from his lips and edged closer to the big man.

'The name's Scattergun,' he informed the blacksmith. 'Scattergun Smith.'

The blacksmith sighed heavily.

'That don't impress me none,' he said drily. 'All I know is that you ain't kindly to this horse of yours.'

A wry smile crossed the hard features of the man sporting the hefty weaponry and ammunition. He shrugged and paced to the barn doors again. He stopped, rested his gloved knuckles on the grips of his double-barrelled guns and stared out beyond the sunlit streets at the sandstorm.

'That storm is getting worse,' he muttered. 'I

74

ain't ever seen its like.'

The blacksmith strode to his side. He sniffed and spat and then stroked his whiskered chin.

'We get a lot of sandstorms in these parts,' he remarked. 'I don't even break a sweat any more when I see them coming.'

Scattergun continued to look at the wall of swirling sand as it swayed in the sky like a genie escaping from the neck of a bottle.

'Is that a bad storm?' he asked.

'It might be,' the hefty man replied. 'It's hard to tell until it passes over the town. Last year we had one which come on us real sudden.'

Scattergun looked at the thoughtful man. 'What happened?'

'It killed a dozen folks and ripped as many buildings off their foundations.' The blacksmith sighed. 'Damn shame. Took the prettiest little whorehouse up into the sky with about five of the handsomest little gals you ever done seen.'

Scattergun Smith felt uneasy at the thought of buildings being torn from the ground and turned to matchwood. He rested a shoulder against one of the barn doors.

'You got a name, big man?' he enquired of the blacksmith.

The blacksmith looked at the heavily armed stranger.

'Sure I got me a name,' he growled. 'They call me Jeb Sharpe, on account of it's my name.'

Scattergun smiled. 'Howdy, Jeb.'

Sharpe rubbed his hands down the front of his leather apron and ambled up to the forge. He looked at his steaming coffee pot on the coals, then glanced at his mysterious client.

'You thirsty?' he asked.

Scattergun followed Sharpe to the forge. 'Yep. I'm thirsty. I swallowed half that desert yonder riding here.'

Sharp grabbed a tin cup off a work bench and shook the debris from it. He then tossed it at the gunfighter before finding himself another tin cup.

'I don't normally share coffee with folks that hurt their horseflesh, but I got me a feeling you ain't gonna do it again, are you?'

'Nope. I swear I'll turn over a new leaf.' Scattergun held the cup by its handle while the blacksmith filled it with the black beverage.

Sharpe filled his own tin mug with coffee and returned the pot to the coals. He sat down and gestured to an upturned water bucket beside him.

'Sit down, Smith.' He blew the steam off his

coffee as his eyes studied the mustang. 'Them guns and bullet-belts must weigh a ton.'

Scattergun sat down. 'I'm on the trail of an outlaw named Bradley Black, Jeb. You ain't heard of him, have you?'

Sharpe nodded and pointed at three stalls at the far end of the livery. 'The grey gelding is his nag. The two brown horses belong to the two young-sters he rode into San Miguel with.'

Scattergun pushed the Stetson off his brow and allowed it to perch on the crown of his head. It was the first time anyone had mentioned that Black was not alone.

'There were three of them?' he queried.

Sharpe smiled. 'You can't be much of a tracker if'n you didn't know that, Smith boy. Black was with two younger men when they reached here. They was mighty fragrant. They stank the stable out. Upset my older horses.'

'I'm only after Black,' Scattergun said. 'I didn't have any notion that he'd hooked up with two cohorts. That kinda changes things.'

'Why you trailing Black?'

There was a long silence while Scattergun stared into the steam as it rose from his cup. Then he returned the watchful blacksmith's gaze.

'I got my reasons for hunting him, Jeb,' he said.

'You a bounty hunter?' Sharpe wondered.

'I ain't after the bounty on Black's head,' Scattergun replied solemnly. 'I've got me other reasons to be hunting him down. Real good reasons.'

'And you ain't gonna tell me.' Sharpe sighed.

'I reckon not, Jeb.'

'You got a grudge to settle, by my figuring,' Sharpe said, holding the tin cup in the palms of his large hands. 'A mighty fearsome grudge by the sound of it.'

Scattergun said nothing, but it was obvious to the blacksmith that he was reliving every dark memory as he sipped at his coffee.

'It'll cost you three dollars,' Sharpe said.

'What will?'

'Tending the mustang for a couple of nights.'

Scattergun fished out a five-dollar gold piece and handed it across the distance between them. Sharpe bit the coin and slipped it into his apron pocket.

'I hope you ain't hankering to get any change, Smith.' He grinned. 'If you are, you're out of luck. I'm plumb out of change.'

'Take good care of that horse and we'll call it

quits.' Scattergun stood up and placed his empty cup on the workbench. 'I reckon I'd best start looking for Black and his cronies before that storm decides to juggle with the buildings around here, Jeb.'

Scattergun tightened his drawstring and touched his hat brim. He walked to the tall doors, paused, then continued out into the blazing sunlight.

Jeb Sharpe reached for his coffee pot and refilled his tin cup. He scratched his whiskery neck and sighed heavily.

'That fella got vinegar,' Sharpe said. 'He'll need every drop of it if he intends getting the better of Black.'

SEVEN

Bo Wax and Festus Pike had left their paymaster with instructions to find the mysterious Scattergun Smith and kill him. As was their way, they intended to do exactly as Judge Johnson had told them. The two guards moved down through the maze of alleyways until they reached the main street. The storm was growing stronger and starting to make its unholy presence felt as well as heard.

Wax leaned against the whitewashed wall of a humble adobe at the end of the town's main thoroughfare and halted his cohort with the palm of his outstretched hand.

Pike rested against his partner and squinted into the raging sandstorm. The street was nearly empty apart from tumbleweed and a few brave souls daring to do their chores.

'What you looking at, Bo?' Pike asked.

'I was looking for the *hombre* that Judge Johnson told us to kill, Festus,' Wax replied. He spat the dust from his mouth.

'But how do you figure on recognizing him?' Pike wondered. 'We ain't ever seen him before.'

'All we gotta do is find a critter that fits his name.'

Festus Pike pulled away from Wax. 'You mean we look for a critter toting a shotgun?'

'Maybe two shotguns, Festus,' Wax replied; he had spotted a tall figure battling against the strong gale that was lashing San Miguel. The guard raised his gunhand and pointed. 'Do you reckon that's him?'

Pike nodded firmly. 'Holy cow! I figure if anyone is Scattergun Smith, it's him.'

Both men straightened up and checked their holstered six-shooters. Then they took a deep breath, walked out into the wide street and stood to face the approaching Scattergun.

The wind buffeted both men as they eyed the unique shooting rig hanging from the man's hips, yet they stood firm.

Scattergun stopped and pulled the brim of his

hat down to shield his eyes from the sand. He stared at the men, whose hands were hovering above their gun grips.

'What do you *hombres* want?' Scattergun asked, sensing that he already knew the answer to his own question.

Wax glanced at Pike and winked.

'Now!' he exclaimed.

Both men drew their guns. Hot lead spewed from their gun barrels and cut across the distance between them and the startled Scattergun. Hot tapers of lethal fury lifted his coat tails as Scattergun dragged one of his guns from its holster and cocked its hammers.

Scattergun pulled on one of his triggers. A huge cloud of gunsmoke encircled the buckshot as it blasted from the shotgun's barrel.

Festus Pike was lifted off the ground by the shot. His lifeless body was thrown backwards as Wax dropped on to one knee and cocked his gun hammer again.

Scattergun pulled hard on his other trigger.

The shotgun jolted in his hand as it violently unleashed its venomous anger at the kneeling Bo Wax.

Through narrowed eyes Scattergun watched as

the second guard vanished into a haze of smoke and blood. Scattergun swallowed hard and pulled the spent cartridges from his shotguns. As he strode towards the bloody remnants of the two guards his gloved fingers slid two fresh shells into his smoking weapons.

Scattergun stared down at the bodies, then glanced up. His gaze darted around the street as tumbleweed and sand rolled over the bloodstained ground.

'What in tarnation is going on here?' he muttered. 'Jeb said that Black had two young critters with him. Neither of these varmints could have ever passed for young.'

Roughly a mile from the limits of San Miguel a rambling rose-covered hacienda stood in an ornate garden. It looked out of place in such a desolate terrain. Few men had ever set foot in the grounds of the large estate and even fewer had ever been invited inside the whitewashed hacienda. This was the domain of General Luis Cordova. Cordova was a highly decorated Mexican officer who had retired only to discover that his army pension was not adequate to keep him in the manner to which he had become accustomed.

The General, as he was known, quickly discovered that his prowess at planning military operations was easily adapted to planning criminal activities. Cordova soon began to reap the profits of his unusual skill.

At first outlaws travelled to San Miguel in order to find the mysterious man known as the General and to profit from his knowledge. Then, as Cordova prospered and his wealth grew to unimaginable heights, he became even more ruthless and cunning. Now he would only deal with outlaws whom he personally had summoned.

Apart from a few domestic servants and his three highly paid *vaqueros*, Cordova lived alone inside his magnificent fortified hacienda. Seclusion gave Cordova the time for his brilliant military brain to calculate every detail of his forthcoming operations.

Unlike many other generals Cordova had never sacrificed his men in battle. The same ethic applied now. If the outlaws followed his detailed instructions they would achieve their goals with the least number of casualties.

His well-armed *vaqueros* ensured that nobody ever rode on to his estate to trouble the General unless they had been invited to do so.

For over three years Cordova had grown to be like a king in a land of peasants. Yet just planning daring bank raids with military precision had become a bore for the General. He needed something new and more demanding to satisfy his relentless appetite for actiion.

Bolder plans grew, like the storm that was raging now. Plans which required execution in order for him to gain the one thing his recent wealth had not yet blessed him with.

Now Cordova desired power.

Sending for the infamous outlaw Bradley Black had been the first step towards achieving his ambition. Cordova knew that there was one man in this arid land who controlled the entire territory. This man spent a few days in San Miguel every month as he toured his vast mining interests.

Judge Cleveland Johnson had everything the General required. Once the judge had been disposed of, Cordova knew exactly how he would use not only his own growing fortune but also the power that Johnson had amassed.

Unlike the General, Johnson did not understand how to exploit his own power. Cordova knew that to usurp it would make him untouchable on both sides of the long border. Sending for the infamous

Bradley Black would be his masterstroke.

Once Black had executed the reviled business-man the General's grand plan could be put into operation with no hint of Cordova's involvement ever being discovered.

The General had not overlooked a single detail. Soon the plan would become a reality. Even though Judge Johnson was well-protected, the General knew that none of his guards could stop Black.

Cordova stood on his veranda and awaited the arrival of the executioner. There was only one thing that troubled the elegant General: the unpredictable storm he now watched closing in on San Miguel.

The sound of horses approaching diverted his attention and the General turned his head. He watched as two of his *vaqueros* came riding towards the hacienda from different directions.

Pancho Sanchez drew rein, dropped from his high-shouldered mount and rushed to Cordova's side.

'Black has arrived in San Miguel, General,' he informed his master.

Cordova nodded and watched as Sanchez's younger brother Benito pulled back on his reins and dismounted.

'Johnson has arrived at his house in town, General,' he gasped.

Both *vaqueros* watched Cordova smile as he imagined how close he was to achieving his goal.

'Soon my most daring of plans will begin, *amigos*,' he told them.

Pancho Sanchez looped his beaded reins to a hitching pole close to the veranda.

'Black was not alone when he arrived in San Miguel, General,' he stated. 'He brought two young men with him.'

The General made a carefree gesture. 'It does not matter, Pancho. They will not interfere with my plans.'

'The storm is getting very bad down there, General,' Benito said, pointing to the distant settlement.

Cordova placed a hand on the *vaquero*'s shoulder.

'Do not worry, Benito,' he said in a fatherly tone. 'I cannot do anything about the storm.'

The three men entered the luxurious interior of the hacienda.

EIGHT

San Miguel had become unusually dark as the storm clouds gathered. The blazing sun was becoming blocked out as the storm drew ever closer to the little border town. Its rays were no longer able to reach the ground where San Miguel stood. The eerie howling noise grew ever louder. The small town was directly in the path of one of nature's more destructive forces; it had already started to feel the buffeting of the relentless winds.

As with all storms, its consequences were unpredictable. There was no way of knowing how much damage it would inflict upon San Miguel. Scattergun, however, was unconcerned about the storm. All he could think about was getting Bradley Black in his sights and ending the outlaw's life, just as he had slain the two guards who now lay a hundred yards behind his spurs.

Scattergun tightened his hat's drawstring and stepped up on to the boardwalk of a hardware store. He rested his shoulder against its porch upright and rubbed the sand from his eyes.

In all his days he had never encountered a storm quite like this one. What had started as a sandstorm was now growing into something else.

Something far more troubling.

With half-closed eyes he watched the funnel of fearsome power twisting up into the sky. He had never before witnessed anything like it. The prophetic words of the blacksmith did not seem so far-fetched now. This tempest was truly capable of tearing houses from their foundations.

Scattergun could feel the storm's strength as invisible gusts swept around the wide street. Roof shingles were ripped off a few of the buildings opposite the spot where Scattergun rested. Once torn free of their nails they simply vanished up into the darkening sky.

The afternoon sun still had many hours to go before setting, yet the storm was doing its best to prevent its fiery brilliance from reaching the ground beneath it. Scattergun gripped the upright firmly and then noticed that nothing in San Miguel was safe from the sheer force of the strange creature that had begun to move eerily across the settlement.

His eyes squinted hard and focused upon buildings swaying like tall grass. It seemed unbelievable to his tired mind.

A couple of saddle horses galloped past Scattergun, their instincts telling them to flee whilst there was still time to do so. He had never seen buildings move before and it unsettled him. What he would have thought to be impossible was really happening. The wooden structures were being shaken by the unbridled fury of the approaching storm, seemingly trying to abandon their very foundations. Only the smaller adobe dwellings appeared to be immune.

Mustering every fibre of his strength, Scattergun pushed himself away from the upright and walked unsteadily along the boardwalk. As he continued defiantly on towards the nearest hotel its hand-painted façade was torn free. Advancing, he thought about Black. The outlaw was in San Miguel, he supposed. And he was not alone. It was more than likely that Black was in the hotel with his underlings. Scattergun's half-closed eyes homed in on the windswept hostelry as he walked on towards it. Suddenly a loud noise from out of the dense cloud of sand made him turn.

Scattergun ducked as the heavy hotel name boards were torn from the balcony. They flew over his head and crashed into the ground a few feet behind him. He staggered onwards to the hotel, where he found another porch upright to cling on to.

He grabbed the upright. It took every scrap of strength but Scattergun managed to force himself up on to the hotel's boardwalk. He was startled but unwilling to quit his hunt.

The double doors of the hotel were only ten feet from him but it might as well have been a mile. He knew that if he released his grip he would be unable to stop himself from being sent cartwheeling down the street. It was all he could do to remain standing on one spot.

Scattergun felt helpless. He had faced many men in his time. Men who wanted nothing more than to kill him. He had never once been afraid of any of them, but this was different.

Memories of his motive for travelling to San Miguel vanished from his mind. All he could think about was the strange forces that tugged at his every sinew. Unseen hands were trying to pull him free of the upright. Pounding fists were tearing into his ribs and chin, but there was nobody there.

A scream from across the street caught his attention. He glanced to where he had heard the sound of the female voice, then he saw a woman being dragged down the centre of the street. He wanted to help her but it was impossible.

Scattergun watched, unable to move, as she slid along the ground, the wind catching her many layers of undergarments. Sand peppered his face like buckshot, and by the time it eased she was gone from view.

Then the loudest of cracking noises made Scattergun look up. The wooden upright he was clinging to split and was violently separated from the balcony it supported.

An explosion of wood and splinters deafened him.

The upright toppled like a felled tree. His gloved hands no longer had anything to hold on to. Scattergun rolled helplessly down the steps of the boardwalk, landed on his back and was blown along the street like tumbleweed. He slid across the sand and might have kept going if he had not collided with a water trough filled with its precious liquid.

He hit the trough hard.

The sound of his head cracking was almost as loud as it was painful. Scattergun lay on his side trying to figure out whether it was the storm he could hear or the war drums inside his aching skull.

He was badly dazed but he was unwilling to remain prostrate in the dirt. He clawed at the wooden side of the trough in an attempt to get back to his feet again. He had almost succeeded when a massive chunk of debris emerged from the swirling sand. It hurtled across the street and crashed into him.

It punched him like a prize fighter.

No jackass could have kicked harder. Scattergun swayed on his knees and toppled on to his face. His eyes flickered but then everything went black as he slumped into a heap.

A whirlpool of nausea seemed to open up and swallow him.

NINE

Cy Russell emerged from the storm and ran past Judge Johnson's carriage and horses in the private stable next to the house. He beat a fist on the side door and waited until his fellow guard Sam Dexter opened up.

Dexter stared at Russell. 'What the hell's wrong, Cy? You look like you seen a ghost.'

Russell pushed his way into the house.

'Where's the judge? I gotta see him right away,' he shouted.

Dexter slammed the door and trailed Russell to where Johnson was sitting with a bottle of wine to one side of him and a plate filled with sliced cheese to the other.

Johnson looked up angrily.

'What the hell are you doing, Cy?' he shouted.

Russell leaned over his boss. 'Festus and Bo are dead, Judge.'

Johnson's face went pale. He stared into the terrified eyes of his guard and swallowed hard.

'Are you sure?' he mumbled.

Russell nodded frantically. 'That Scattergun critter blasted them apart, Judge. They're spread across Main Street from one side to the other.'

Slowly Johnson rose to his feet. Neither of these two guards had ever seen their employer look quite so troubled before. He walked slowly to the window and stared out at the unearthly view.

'So Scattergun Smith is dangerous, huh?' he mulled. 'It don't matter none. I'll pay you boys a thousand dollars apiece if you bring me his damn head.'

Johnson faced his two remaining men.

'Are you willing?' he asked.

Russell and Dexter looked at one another. They exchanged malevolent grins before they both nodded at their paymaster.

Johnson moved between his guards.

'Go *kill* the bastard,' he hissed.

*

The sandstorm had almost covered the motionless Scattergun Smith by the time Bradley Black led Dade Coleman and Keno Mason out from the refuge of their hotel. The outlaws were clean and sporting new trail gear as they braved the windswept street. The unmistakable aroma of carbolic soap wafted in their wake. They battled against the blinding sand and powerful winds; not even an impending hurricane could have stopped them.

Black led Mason and Coleman towards the livery stable at the far end of town. It was not as easy to reach it as it had been when they had first arrived in the parched settlement.

The trio reached the big building and managed to fight their way inside it. Sand whistled eerily through the gaps in the cladding and spooked even the calmest of horses. Black spat and rubbed the sand from his hardened features as his eyes searched for the stalwart blacksmith. Mason and Coleman stood beside the veteran outlaw and dusted themselves down.

'Where in tarnation are you, big man?' Black yelled.

For such a large creature, Jeb Sharpe had an unlikely knack of finding every nook and cranny within his livery capable of secreting his bulk. He emerged from behind his forge with a set of long tongs resting on his shoulder.

Mason and Coleman swung on their heels, drew their six-shooters and aimed them at the muscular blacksmith. Sharpe picked up his tin cup and drained it of coffee.

'Your pups are a tad nervous, Black,' Sharpe remarked.

Black lowered his head and grinned at the blacksmith. He glanced at his men.

'Holster them .45s, boys,' he ordered. 'It ain't friendly pointing guns at a man as big as he is.'

Reluctantly the pair of young outlaws did as they were told. Black strode to the forge and warmed his hands over its glowing coals.

'Has Scattergun Smith paid you a visit, Jeb?' Black asked the large man. 'We seen someone headed here earlier who I figured looked a lot like that scum-sucking bastard.'

Sharpe removed the tongs from his shoulder and set them on the brickwork of his forge. He then refilled his cup with well-brewed coffee and lifted it to his lips.

'Yep, I've had me a visitation. He arrived here a while after you left your horses, Black,' Sharpe calmly replied.

Black tilted his head and eyed the blacksmith. 'Where'd he go? Did he buy a new horse and light out, or did he figure on staying in San Miguel?'

Sharpe stared through the steam rising from his tin cup at the old outlaw's face.

'He left his horse to rest up from the punishment it endured getting here. I ain't seen him since.' He smiled wryly.

Black looked thoughtful. 'Knowing Scattergun he's waiting in one of the saloons in town to get a sight of me,' he said knowingly.

'He did look a tad thirsty.' Sharpe nodded.

Bradley Black stepped closer to the brawny blacksmith.

'What did he tell you?' he growled.

Unfazed by the outlaw's aggression, Sharpe took a mouthful of the hot beverage, then lowered his cup.

'Scattergun said he was hunting you, Black,' he blacksmith replied. 'I asked if he was a bounty hunter but he didn't seem interested in the reward on your head. He said he had himself another reason for hunting you. What could that be, Black?'

As the storm still buffeted the building, Black turned away from the blacksmith. He pointed at their horses.

'Saddle my horse up, Jeb,' he drawled. 'I have some business to attend to.'

Sharpe tossed his cup down beside the coffee pot and ambled towards the stalls. He grabbed a blanket off a stall wall and draped it across the grey.

'Ain't the weather to go riding, Black,' he commented, his big hand patting the blanket flat on the gelding's back. 'By my reckoning that breeze out there is strong enough to lift a man and his horse off the ground and toss them clean away.'

Sharpe picked up Black's saddle and placed it on top of the mount's back. He bent over, reached under the animal's belly and pulled the cinch towards him.

'Just hurry up, Jeb,' Black said. 'I'm in a hurry.'

'Where you figuring on going, Black?' Sharpe asked. He tightened the cinch and then secured it.

Black rested one hand on his gun grip and the other on the hairy shoulder of the greasy blacksmith. Each man locked his gaze on to the other's.

'Don't get too curious, Jeb,' Black warned.

Sharpe shrugged, then lowered the stirrup and fender.

'I ain't curious, Black,' he said, handing the reins to the outlaw. 'I was just making small talk.'

'Don't,' Black snarled. 'You'll live longer that way.'

Black led the grey across the floor of the livery towards his cohorts. He looked at his men.

'While I'm away from town rustling up business I want you to find and kill Scattergun, boys.' Black rammed his left boot into the stirrup and mounted.

Coleman opened one of the large stable doors against the severe gusts of wind. He looked up at Black.

'We'll bushwhack the varmint,' he said.

'Good. I'd hate for you boys to make the mistake of facing his shotguns,' Black said. 'Just find his sorrowful hide and cut him to ribbons in your crossfire. Savvy?'

'We savvy, Brad,' Mason said.

They watched Black spur his grey and ride out into the blinding sand storm. He was heading in the direction of the hacienda.

Coleman nudged Mason. 'Let's get out of here, Keno,' He muttered.

Sharpe walked across the livery and closed the tall door behind his departing unwelcome guests. He spat at the floor and ambled back to the forge.

TEN

The force of the storm was at its zenith. The fast-moving air was not only filled with blinding sand but also chunks of debris. Entire buildings had been razed to the ground and yet the storm's appetite was still ravenous. By the time Scattergun regained consciousness he was almost completely buried in sand deposited by the spine-chilling wind. The noise of its howling woke Scattergun from his enforced slumber and dragged him back into consciousness. For a moment he had no notion of where he was or how he had come to be there. All he knew for sure was that he was drowning.

Drowning in an ocean of choking sand.

Panic suddenly enveloped him. His hands moved to his face and swiftly clawed the fine granules from his eyes and nose. He turned on to his side and coughed. Finally he managed to suck enough air into his lungs to breathe.

Scattergun attempted to remember what had happened to him. Slowly he recalled the moment when something large had collided with his skull. The pain had been brief but now it was back with a vengeance. His head hurt. It hurt worse than he had ever imagined possible.

Thunder and lightning fought for supremacy inside his pounding skull. Scattergun coughed in an effort to clear the sand and debris from his lungs, then he recalled trying to get to the hotel in order to find out whether Black and his hirelings were holed up there.

The storm had had other ideas. Now he was on his hands and knees staring at the ground like a whipped dog. Scattergun narrowed his eyes until they were virtually closed in a vain attempt to see.

It was nearly impossible.

The storm had made the afternoon sun disappear from view. Now it lingered in the very heart of San Miguel like a demonic vulture. It had not finished its destruction yet and Scattergun knew that

103

it had probably not satisfied its lust for killing, either.

His hand shakily grabbed the rim of the water trough. He fought against the powerful wind until he was standing once more. The storm rocked him but he refused to be budged while his hands instinctively moved down to his hips and satisfied themselves that his shotguns were still holstered.

He looked around again but still could not see a thing.

The dense cloud of swirling sand cut into him as he staggered to where he knew the nearest building stood. He tripped and fell under the porch as the screaming sirens of the relentless havoc mocked him.

It was like being blind, he thought.

Blind and helpless.

Scattergun patted the brick portion of the lower wall and managed to get back to his feet. His gloved hands were now his eyes.

A desperate thought occurred to him.

Bradley Black was somewhere in San Miguel. He did not want to encounter the infamous outlaw without being able to see him. Death was always close but Scattergun did not relish meeting it blindly.

Scattergun pressed his back against the wall and gathered his thoughts. He steadied himself. It was not easy. Scattergun had no idea of where he was apart from the fact that he had been close to the hotel before being knocked out.

His eyes stared at the swirling sand before him. It was like looking at a monstrous creature which stung his eyes like a million hornets. Scattergun had to shield his eyes if he was to have a chance of opening them wide enough to see without being punished for trying.

Then he remembered the feed sack in his pocket. The sack he had retrieved from his saddle-bags in the livery stable earlier.

The sack had worked earlier. Maybe it would work now. One hand loosened the drawstring of his hat whilst the other pulled the crude sack from his pocket. Scattergun quickly removed his Stetson and placed the sack over his head. He then replaced the hat and tightened its drawstring until it nearly throttled him.

Still pinned against the wall he adjusted the sacking until the two eyeholes were where they were meant to be. For a moment he still could not see anything. Then, as the sacking stopped the sand from tearing into his eyes, he was able to just make out a few blurred objects.

Scattergun was determined to remain on his feet this time. As he felt the blood start to pump furiously in his veins again he recalled why he had ridden for so long in pursuit of Bradley Black.

He had never wanted to claim the price on the outlaw's head. There was another reason why he intended killing Black.

A far greater reason.

Black was a train robber and a brutal killer. Some said that he was an expert with his six-shooter. Every single reason that others might have had to slay the evil outlaw meant nothing to Scattergun.

He had a far purer reason for wanting Black dead.

His desire to execute the infamous outlaw was personal.

The storm eased for a few moments. It was all he needed to encourage him. Scattergun stared along the street and spotted Mason and Coleman staggering down the centre of the wide thoroughfare.

He had no idea who they were as he watched their approach. Scattergun wondered if they knew where he might find Black; he decided to ask if either of them had seen the deadly outlaw.

Feeling as though he was in the most horrific of nightmares the tall figure forced his bruised and aching body away from the wall, stepped down from the boardwalk and walked towards the pair of approaching outlaws.

Unlike the man with the feed sack shield over his head Keno Mason and Dade Coleman had only their hands to protect their eyes from the blinding sand that still tormented them from every angle.

The brief lull in the storm was short-lived.

The snorting beast soon resumed its chaotic tantrum.

Undeterred, Scattergun reached the middle of the street and stopped. He waited for the pair of equally forlorn men to reach him as the intensity of the tempest grew. With the tails of his coat pushed over his shotguns' grips, he watched them approach.

At first neither outlaw noticed the daunting apparition until they were within twenty feet of him. Coleman stopped first and grabbed the arm of his cohort in terror.

'Lookee yonder, Keno,' he shouted above the sound of the howling wind. 'What in tarnation is that?'

Mason stopped and screwed up his eyes.

'Holy cow!' he gasped fearfully as his eyes focused on the strange hooded man. 'That critter ain't got no face like normal folks. What the hell is that?'

Coleman noticed the two shotguns on the hips of the man who faced them. He raised a shaking hand and pointed.

'He might not have no face but he's got himself scatterguns, Keno,' he stammered. Then the raging of the storm diminished their ability to see Smith clearly any longer. 'That's the varmint Brad told us about. He's the bastard he told us to kill.'

'Oh, hell!' Mason cursed. 'Brad never told us he was some kinda monster.'

'That ain't no monster, Keno,' Coleman said. 'Whatever he is, he ain't no monster.'

Mason felt terror race through his body. The strange sight in front of him was unlike anything he had ever imagined. The mighty gusts of wind moved the hemp sacking that protected Scattergun's face. It created a sight which was unlike anything remotely mortal.

'That's gotta be him, Dade,' Mason yelled out piteously as he vainly attempted to convince himself. 'Look at them damn guns.'

'You're right, Keno.' Coleman nodded in agreement. 'That's Scattergun Smith.'

Hearing his name, Scattergun realized that the two men in front of him were not townsfolk. They had to be the pair who had joined the notorious Black on the trail. The awesome figure raised his arms until his hands hovered just above the stocks of the holstered twin-barrelled shotguns.

'Where's Black?' he shouted out at the two terrified men.

The outlaws tried to shield their unsteady bodies from the wind which kept tormenting them. It was not an easy task. Yet no matter how much the storm buffeted them it seemed that Scattergun did not move. Only the tails of his coat flapped in reply to the incessant battering.

Otherwise the hooded man seemed totally unaffected.

Mason screwed up his red-raw eyes and studied the target he intended hitting with every bullet in his .45. He pointed an accusing finger.

'You Scattergun Smith?' he shouted.

Scattergun did not answer. He kept watching the two outlaws through the jagged holes in his woven hemp mask, knowing that at any moment they would go for their weapons.

Coleman carefully rested his shaking hand on his holstered six-shooter and glared at the faceless man before them. His finger slid around the gun's trigger. He hoped that the swaying wall of blinding sand would hide his actions from the ominous figure.

'Of course that's Scattergun, Keno,' he snarled.

The young outlaw took a step forward.

'Why are you hunting Brad Black?' he raged. 'Are you a stinking bounty hunter?'

Scattergun remained perfectly motionless as every sinew in his bruised body fought the unrelenting wind and abrasive sand, which had already demolished several of the less sturdy buildings that surrounded them.

Coleman grew as nervous as his young saddle pal.

'Answer, damn you!' he screamed out.

Scattergun knew they were close to drawing their guns and unloading their bullets in his direction. He raised his head and peered through the holes in the sacking.

'Yep, I'm Scattergun Smith,' he confirmed. 'I ain't no bounty hunter though.'

Mason was confused. 'Then why are you hunting down Black?'

'Simple. I intend killing him. Just like I'll have to kill you two unless you turn tail and ride out of San

Miguel, boy.' Scattergun replied in a low tone. 'I'm giving you the chance of living, boys. You can reject my offer if you want. It's up to you 'coz I don't give a hoot.'

Coleman glanced at Mason.

'You figure he's serious?' he asked.

Mason shook his head. 'Nope, he's lying. He'll shoot us in the back as soon as we turn, Dade.'

'That's what you'd do, sonny,' Scattergun shouted at them. 'Don't make the mistake of thinking everyone sings from the same hymn sheet. I'm no back-shooter.'

The swaying outlaws held their ground.

'I don't trust him, Keno,' Coleman said. His fingers gripped his holstered .45.

'Me neither. He's lying, I tell you,' Mason screamed in hysterical fury. 'Nobody lets outlaws just ride away. He's a stinking bounty hunter, I tell you. A back-shooting bounty hunter.'

Scattergun tilted his head and sighed.

'Then draw and die,' he said. 'It don't make no difference to me.'

Before Coleman could say or do another thing, his young companion had hauled his six-shooter from its holster. Before Mason had had time to cock the hammer of the .45 Scattergun had drawn

111

his own impressive weapons from their specially designed holsters.

The lethal sawn-off shotgun in his left hand blasted as Scattergun squeezed on its triggers. The explosion of fiery venom erupted from its twin barrels and carved a path through the choking air. Within a mere heartbeat Keno Mason was dead. Only his lower half survived the buckshot as it obliterated the outlaw.

Coleman watched in stunned horror as the young outlaw was shredded into bits not ten feet from him. Instinctively he drew his own six-shooter and trained it on the mysterious figure who stood holding both his shotguns in his hands. Smoke billowed from one of the big weapons, but the shotgun in his right hand had yet to be fired.

As Coleman fanned the hammer of his .45 he saw Scattergun raise his fearsome weapon. It was the last thing Dade Coleman ever saw. The deafening blasts that spewed from the barrels of the shotgun found their target easily.

Flesh and bone were torn from the outlaw's body and scattered in the storm.

The remnants of the outlaws lay in pools of crimson gore. Scattergun snapped his guns open. He sent spent shells flying to either side of him, then he expertly inserted fresh cartridges from the belts that crossed his chest.

Scattergun jerked both guns upward. Their mighty barrels locked back into position before he dropped them into their holsters on his hips once more.

The hooded man felt no satisfaction at the sight of his bloody handiwork. Then a burning sensation in his left shoulder began to torment him. He touched the wound. He looked through the holes in his mask, staring silently at the smouldering bullet hole. The fabric of his coat's shoulder had been blackened by the outlaw's bullet: a bullet that had gone straight through his flesh. Scattergun watched as blood started to trickle from the hole.

At least one of the dead outlaws had been fast, he thought. Not fast enough, though. Scattergun ignored the wound and looked at the brutal finality he had created.

Neither Coleman nor Mason had answered his first question. Scattergun still did not know where the infamous Bradley Black was. For reasons he could not understand, the two young men had died rather than spill the beans. They were either loyal to Black or just plain dumb.

The tall hooded man strode forward through

the bloody debris and was then engulfed by the unholy cloud of merciless sand, which still blocked out the afternoon sun. The sandstorm appeared to be getting worse.

Even with his head covered by the hemp sacking he could still smell the aftermath of his actions. The sickening stench of gunsmoke filled his nostrils.

Scattergun lowered his head, defied the storm and moved on towards the livery stable. With each step he wondered why he could detect the aroma of carbolic soap on the savage wind. He looked up and saw the faint brightness of the sun vainly trying to penetrate the storm cloud.

Scattergun stopped when he reached the livery stable. The sound of distressed horses inside the storm-battered building greeted his ears. He walked to the big doors and tried them. They were locked from inside. Scattergun raised a gloved fist and pounded upon them.

'Open up, Jeb,' he bellowed.

ELEVEN

It was difficult to hear anything over the sound of the storm and the trampling of the skittish horses, yet the muscular blacksmith did hear something that alerted his attention. He looked up from his coffee cup. He placed it on the forge. At first the sound of pounding on the stables' doors blended in with the constant noise of the storm, which bellowed as if to enter and destroy the ramshackle building. Only when the blacksmith heard the voice of the mysterious stranger did he rise from his chair and march quickly to the secured doors. Although he had only heard Scattergun's voice once, it was memorable. There was something about the accent which sounded unlike any other.

Jeb Sharpe's strong hands dragged the bolt

across the doors and he ushered Scattergun inside.
Sharpe frowned as the hooded figure entered and
passed by him, but it was obvious who he had
allowed to come into his stable. The burly blacksmith bolted the doors, then turned to follow his
unexpected visitor.

As Sharpe followed the tall figure towards the
warmth of the forge he noticed the blood dripping
down his trail coat from the exit wound in
Scattergun's shoulder.

'Thanks for letting me back in, Jeb,' Scattergun
said.

'Are you OK, boy?' Sharpe asked. He watched
Scattergun remove his hat and mask, then rest
wearily against the forge. 'You got a bullet hole in
you.'

Scattergun glanced at Sharpe.

'I'm sure glad you told me that, Jeb,' he
grunted. 'I just thought I'd bin stung by a bee.'

Sharpe brushed the sarcasm aside.

'Take that dumb hood off your head, boy,' he
growled, pushing Scattergun down on to the
makeshift seat. He pointed a large finger at him.
'Now sit there and don't say another word.'

'What you figuring on doing, Jeb?' Scattergun
asked.

'I'm gonna tend that wound, boy,' Sharpe told him. 'Any objections?'

'Nope, not a one.'

The grey gelding had made good time since it had left San Miguel and the raging storm. Brad Black glanced back at the border town and grinned as he travelled through the sun-drenched countryside. The storm was still torturing the settlement but showed no sign of turning in his direction. He whipped the tails of his long leathers over his mount's shoulders and encouraged the feisty animal on towards the hacienda.

As the grey thundered on to the magnificent dwelling Black began to wonder why the famed Mexican general had sent for him. He had never before heard of Cordova summoning the likes of him. Usually it was the outlaws who got in touch with him to plan their robberies for them.

Cordova needed Black for some unknown reason.

Someone needed killing, the infamous outlaw kept telling himself. Some poor galoot did not know it yet, but his time was running out.

The horse kept on running as its master brooded about the reasons behind his being summoned by Luis Cordova, given that the military man could gather an army by simply snapping his fingers.

Mexicans would lay down their very lives for Cordova. Yet the general had sent for Black. What did Cordova want him to do? It had to involve killing, Black reasoned. Yet why send for a wanted outlaw and not use one of the thousands of loyal soldiers he had commanded over the years?

It made no sense to the outlaw.

Who did he want to be killed? Whoever it was, it had to be somebody important if Cordova was willing to hire a total stranger to do his dirty work for him.

Black spurred and encouraged the grey up a sandy rise. Then he drew back on his leathers and held the snorting animal in check as he studied the hacienda more carefully.

He had never seen anything quite so splendid before. Within its whitewashed adobe walls lurked a man who was well known to the outlaws who plied their trade on both sides of the border. Cordova often used Americans rather than Mexicans to rob banks and trains. By all accounts the General had grown wealthy because he used his knowledge of military campaigning with an expertise few could match.

The notorious outlaw raised himself in his stirrups and stared at the impressive building. In all his days he had never seen a house quite like it.

Few men outside his line of business would have imagined that a criminal genius lived in such an elegant, secluded residence. It confused Black as he gathered up his long leathers.

There was only one way he would learn why he had been sent for, he thought. He gritted his discoloured teeth and whipped a flank of his mount. The grey obeyed its brutal master. It moved through the blisteringly hot terrain at speed. Dust rose from its hoofs. Black eyed every inch of the fenced estate, looking for the guards that he knew Cordova employed. Men like Cordova always hid behind heavily armed protectors.

Black steered the gelding between cactus and sage bushes towards the peaceful-looking hacienda.

The sun blazed down as the grey reached the estate's boundary posts. Black eased back on his reins and glared at the three *vaqueros* who greeted him. They had appeared from seemingly nowhere and each toted a highly polished Winchester in his hands.

No sooner had Black stopped his mount's

progress than the three rifles were swung around and aimed in his direction.

Black looked at the guards in turn and knew that these were no ordinary riflemen. They might have been dressed like *vaqueros* but they were obviously military men.

Trying to conceal his concern, Black leaned over the grey's mane and watched the three *vaqueros* as they cocked their weapons and walked towards him. The highly polished metal barrels gleamed as the sun danced along their lengths.

'I'm expected,' Black grunted.

Pancho Sanchez reached the nose of the grey and studied the outlaw carefully without lowering his rifle.

'Who is expecting you, *señor*?' Sanchez asked, aiming the barrel of his rifle up at the horseman. 'This is private property.'

'Read this.' Black pulled out a telegraph message from his pocket and handed it down to the stony-faced vaquero. Pancho Sanchez kept one eye on the horseman as he glanced at the paper.

He studied the wire intently, then returned it to the horseman. He walked around the grey, then signalled to his two companions.

'Let him through, *amigos*,' he instructed. 'The

General is expecting this gringo.'

The *vaqueros* parted and allowed the grey to walk between them. Nevertheless, as the horse continued on towards the hacienda Black knew that their rifles were still trained upon his back.

As the grey reached a doorway, which had been concealed by a profusion of climbing red roses, Black saw an elegant Mexican step out on to a tiled patio. It was obvious that this was the General, for the man stood with an almost regal nobility. Even though Black had never met Cordova he realized that this must be the legendary military man.

Black hauled back on his reins. The grey stopped. The General and the hardened killer looked at one another. There was an unspoken respect between the two very different men.

The outlaw stared down at the elegant man and touched his hat brim in salute. Cordova acknowledged the deadly killer for whom he had sent.

'It is good to see you, Señor Black,' Cordova said, eyeing the rider.

'How'd you know that I'm Black, General?' Black asked curiously.

'Simple. My *vaqueros* would have killed you if you had been anyone else,' Cordova replied.

Black glanced at the three *vaqueros*, then

returned his stare to the General. A smile played over his face.

'I like your style,' he complimented his host.

'The hills are littered with inquisitive men who tried to breach my privacy, Señor Black,' Cordova said, watching as the outlaw dismounted and tied his reins to a fence pole. 'My men allowed you entry because I had instructed them to do so. You have a skill for which I am willing to pay highly.'

'I'm curious as to why you sent for me,' Black answered. He stepped out of the blazing sunshine into the shade of the arched porch. 'It seems like you've got enough talent without sending for outside help.'

'*Sí, señor.*' Cordova smiled. 'But I require your special abilities.'

Black took a deep breath as he studied the man before him. He decided to take the bull by the horns and ask a straight question.

'You need someone killed, General?' Black asked bluntly. He pulled a cigar from his shirt and placed it between his teeth. 'I got me a feeling that killing is the only real skill I've got that folks like you would be willing to pay for.'

Cordova nodded. 'Indeed. You are correct in you assumption as to why I sent for you, Señor

Black. I need a man killed.'

'That'll cost you plenty,' Black said. He ignited a match with his thumbnail and cupped its flame. 'I'm expensive, but by the looks of it you can afford my price.'

The General tilted his head. 'You arrived in San Miguel with two fellow outlaws, I understand. Do not worry, you will be paid enough to satisfy your overheads.'

Black raised an eyebrow and exhaled a line of smoke at the ground. 'You're well informed, General.'

'I have spies everywhere.' Cordova grinned.

'Let's talk money,' Black said.

'Come with me.' Luis Cordova turned and led Black into the cool interior of the hacienda. 'We shall discuss your fee over fine brandy.'

Black trailed the elegant man into the hacienda. Their footsteps echoed around the impressive interior. The outlaw gazed in awe at the ornate decoration. The walls were covered in trophies. Swords of every shape and size as well as rich tapestries covered the white surfaces.

'This is one hell of a home,' the outlaw remarked.

'I am pleased that you are impressed,' the General replied.

The outlaw followed Cordova into a rectangular room where an oak desk was surrounded by plush chairs of various designs. Black looked up at the vaulted wooden ceiling and was impressed by a beautiful crystal chandelier hanging from a long black chain.

'Sit down, Señor Black.' Cordova gestured to a chair at the desk. 'Would gold coin be suitable?'

Black nodded. 'Gold coin will be just fine, General.'

Smoke trailed from Black's mouth as he slowly lowered himself on to the sturdy chair. He rested a hand on the grip of one of his guns and watched as the General plucked a grape from a silver fruit bowl and devoured it.

'Do not be nervous, Señor Black.' Cordova smiled as he poured two generous measures of brandy into glasses. 'I shall not harm you.'

'I ain't nervous, General,' Black replied. 'I'm just curious. I still don't understand why you need me when you've got three *vaqueros* outside who look able and willing to kill any critter you pointed a finger at.'

'My men are loyal and would do anything I asked them to do, but they are also well known.' Cordova explained. 'If they were recognized killing anyone, people would know that I must have ordered the assassination.'

Cordova placed one glass before Black and warmed the other in the palms of his hands before sitting down opposite the gunman. He inhaled the fragrant fumes of the fine brandy and watched his guest carefully.

'You understand?' he asked. He pulled out a small leather bag from a drawer in his desk and slid it across the varnished surface.

Black picked up the small bag and weighed it in his hand. He smiled at the General.

'Yep, I understand,' he said.

'I shall pay you three thousand dollars in gold coin for your prowess with your guns,' Cordova said. 'Half of which you will find in the sack.'

Black sat upright on his chair. 'That's a lot more than you said in the wire.'

'You shall receive the rest when you have completed the job, Señor Black.' The General grinned and sipped his fine cognac. 'Is that acceptable?'

Black pushed the small sack of coins into his pocket. 'That is real acceptable, General.'

Cordova smiled. 'All I demand of you is that you are discreet. My name must never be mentioned.'

Black took a gulp of his drink and rested his

arms on the desk. He stared at the elegant man opposite him.

'Understood, General,' he said, then asked. 'Now where is the varmint you want me to kill?'

'Your target is in San Miguel, Señor Black,' Cordova replied. 'He arrived earlier with his entourage of guards.'

'How many guards?' Black sucked smoke into his lungs as he awaited the answer.

'Four.'

Black blew smoke across the desk. 'Four guards might hinder most folks, but not me. That's why I brought two young bucks with me. Your victim will be killed no matter how many guards he has surrounding him.'

Cordova placed his glass down and handed a scrap of paper across the table.

'The name of your target is here, as well as his address,' he said.

Black glanced at the note and then pocketed the paper.

'He's as good as dead, General,' he assured his host.

Cordova stood up. He moved to the sculpted fireplace and rested a hand upon its cool surface. 'We have nothing else to say until your triumphant return, Señor Black.'

Black downed the rest of his brandy and stood up. He left the room and retraced his steps to where he had left his grey.

His steps echoed as he strode back into the blazing sunshine and approached his horse. He rubbed his chin, then tugged his leathers free.

Black mounted in one fluid action and gathered his reins in his hands. He turned the horse and rammed his spurs into its flanks. The grey galloped away from the hacienda, quickly gathering pace as it carried its rider back to San Miguel.

The sound of the *vaquero*'s boots echoed around the interior of the hacienda as Pancho Sanchez made his way to where the General was waiting beside the beautiful overmantel.

Cordova raised his eyes and watched as Sanchez entered the room with his sombrero clutched in his hands. The *vaquero* made his way to the side of his beloved general. Each man looked at the other; then Cordova spoke.

'Take your brother and follow Black, Pancho.'

'*Sí*, General.' Sanchez nodded firmly.

Cordova poured another glass of cognac and inhaled its fumes sensuously. He glanced at the *vaquero*.

'When he has completed his task I want you to kill him, Sanchez,' Cordova said. He sighed. 'I do not trust that gringo. He looks as if he will tell of my connection with the death of Judge Johnson. This I cannot allow.'

A wide grin spread across the *vaquero*'s face.

'Do not worry, General. Señor Black will never leave San Miguel alive,' Sanchez vowed.

Cordova sipped his brandy. He listened as the *vaquero's* boot-steps resounded through the house as Sanchez made his way back to the courtyard.

TWELVE

Scattergun Smith focused his gaze on the brawny Jeb Sharpe and nodded firmly. He sighed, then shook his head as he watched the blacksmith return the long poker to the hot coals. The painful operation was over. Sharpe had stemmed the flow of blood by sealing the wound.

Scattergun glanced out of the corner of his eye. 'I should thank you, Jeb. Trouble is I can still smell melting flesh.'

Sharpe filled two cups with fresh coffee and handed one to Scattergun. 'Drink this and relax, boy. You've quit bleeding, ain't you?'

The younger man got back to his feet and steadied himself against the wall. He stared into his steaming coffee and then downed it swiftly. He shuddered.

'Thanks, big man,' he sighed.

Sharpe grinned and helped Scattergun with his shirt. 'I reckon you must be a lot tougher than you look, boy. I don't think I could have remained awake with some *hombre* melting my flesh with a red-hot poker.'

Fighting his desire to buckle, Scattergun tucked his bloodstained shirt into his pants and draped his twin ammunition belts over his chest. The blacksmith handed the trail coat to his unsteady friend and watched as Scattergun slid his arms into its sleeves.

'How do I look?' Scattergun asked.

Sharpe exhaled. 'You don't look good.'

'Maybe you should have let me drink some of that whiskey you poured over my wound.' Scattergun forced a grin. 'I got me a notion that being drunk might help a man who's having his flesh melted by a poker.'

'You could be right.' The blacksmith nodded.

Scattergun frowned as he watched the black-smith with the coffee cup in his large paw. He blinked hard and then listened to the war drums inside his pounding head. He rubbed his temples.

'I got me a whole lot of Apaches inside my head, Jeb,' He said. 'They're beating their damn drums real loud.'

'Have some more coffee.' Sharpe filled the cup in the man's shaking hand. He watched as Scattergun again gulped down its contents. 'Better?'

'A lot better.' Scattergun sighed.

Sharpe raised his bushy eyebrows.

'What you figuring on doing now?' he asked.

'What you mean?'

'You told me that you killed the two galoots Black rode into town with,' Sharpe said. 'Are you in shape to tackle Black when he returns?'

Scattergun tilted his head back and looked at the burly figure as he poured himself another cup of the strong black beverage.

'I reckon I will be when I've walked off the noise in my skull,' he said. He picked up the empty whiskey bottle and looked at it. 'It's a crying shame you wasted the last few drops of this whiskey cleaning out my wound, Jeb.'

'You headed back to the Long Branch?' the blacksmith asked, and smiled as he watched Scattergun place the empty bottle next to the tin cup on the edge of the forge.

'I reckon I am,' Scattergun said. 'I've a powerful thirst and I sure don't want to face Black in this condition.'

'Sober, you mean?'

Scattergun grinned. 'Yeah, sober.'

The blacksmith glanced up at the rafters as granules of fine sand filtered through their gaps.

'The storm is easing up, boy,' he said.

Scattergun looked at his companion. 'Are you sure?'

'Yep, the worst is over,' Sharpe replied confidently. 'In another hour this'll be just a bad memory.'

'A lot of things can happen in an hour, Jeb.'

Sharpe stared at the younger man and frowned. 'What exactly are you, Scattergun? You say that you ain't a bounty hunter but you just killed two varmints out there.'

'I only kill the varmints who are trying to kill me, Jeb,' he said. 'Black is the exception, though.'

'Black is a different kettle of fish, ain't he?' Sharpe asked. 'You come here to San Miguel intending killing him, Scattergun. What makes you want to kill Black so bad?'

'Black is different,' Scattergun said. 'I'm repaying him for what he did to someone I knew.'

'Revenge?' Sharpe sighed.

'That's what they call it.' Scattergun rubbed his eyes.

The blacksmith got back to his feet and ambled to the side of the younger man. He tried to make eye contact but Scattergun diverted his stare from the stalwart figure.

'What did he do to hurt you so bad, boy?' Sharpe eventually asked. 'It must have been plumb awful.'

'What do you mean?'

'It takes something awful to make a man turn his back on the values he's lived his life by, boy,' Sharpe growled. 'You say that you only kill critters that are trying to kill you. Then how come you intend killing Black? What did he do?'

Scattergun groomed his dark hair with the palm of his hand and then placed his hat on his head.

'Thank you kindly for tending my wounds,' he said. He turned on his heel and started towards the big doors. 'Now I've got to find Bradley Black and kill him.'

Sharpe followed Scattergun to the doors and released the bolt. He glanced at the shotgun-toting man beside him.

'You ain't gonna find him in San Miguel, boy.'

Scattergun raised an eyebrow. 'I ain't?'

'He rode out,' Sharpe told him.

'He'll be back,' Scattergun drawled. 'And I'll be waiting.'

Sharpe raised his huge hands and tried to slow Scattergun's progress. 'Tell me. Why are you so damn set on killing that bastard, boy? Why?'

Scattergun suddenly stopped and looked at Sharpe. There was pain etched in the drifter's face and it had nothing to do with the injury he had suffered. Something else was causing the colour to drain from his face.

He looked at Sharpe seriously and then sighed, as though weary of explaining his motives.

'He killed folks that I loved, Jeb,' Scattergun said. 'By my reckoning that bastard has to pay.'

The blacksmith was surprised to be told this much, but he knew there was more. Sharpe tilted his head and studied the younger man carefully. He figured that no one had managed to draw so much information out of the mysterious Scattergun before.

'Who did Black kill?' he asked.

It was obvious that just speaking about his grief was torturous for Scattergun. He lowered his head and stared at his deadly guns. The words that passed his lips were laboured.

'OK, I'll tell you. About a year ago Black showed up in a small town and decided to rob its only bank,' Scattergun began. 'The trouble was Black killed every man, woman and child inside that bank.'

'Everyone?' Sharpe gasped.

'Every precious one of them, Jeb.'

Sharpe straightened up and stared at Scattergun. He looked long and hard, but was unable to ask any more questions.

There was a long pause as Scattergun composed himself in order to finish his explanation. He patted Sharpe's broad shoulder and his next words were whispered.

'Two of them were my wife and child, Jeb,' Scattergun managed to reveal. Then he walked out into the sandstorm's final throes.

Jeb Sharpe closed the stable doors and secured them with the iron bolt. He walked slowly back to the forge as the words of the younger man burned into him like a branding-iron.

His huge hand picked up the coffee pot and he filled his cup. He returned the pot to the coals and sat down. He picked up his tin cup and stared at the black coffee. The steam filled his flared nostrils as he pondered the information he had just learned.

'Kill him, Scattergun,' he muttered angrily. 'You got the right to do that, boy.'

THIRTEEN

Dexter and Russell moved like ravenous cougars through the lanes and alleyways that led from Johnson's house to the very heart of San Miguel. The unearthly sound of the storm had faded but something else had replaced its doomladen howling Now a deadly silence filled the stubborn remains of the little town. It was as if the townsfolk were holding their breath in fear of the storm's return.

Russell turned into an alley with Dexter close on his heels. Both guards drew their Colts and cocked their hammers as they ran towards the end of Main Street.

They stopped.

Fitful wisps of sand still fell like rain. Dexter

pointed his six-shooter at a distant figure who was carefully making his way towards them.

'Is that him?' Dexter asked. 'Is that the critter Judge Johnson told us to kill?'

Russell bit his lip and spat at the boardwalk. His eyes narrowed and focused on the daunting figure. His gaze fixed on the gleaming pair of holstered shotguns as the sun danced across their metal surfaces.

'That has to be him, Sam,' he said drily. 'Look at them guns he's got strapped to his hips.'

Dexter's face went pale in spite of the sun's scorching rays.

'So that's the bastard who killed Bo and Festus,' he railed. 'He sure don't look like any gunfighter I've ever seen before.'

'It ain't his face that troubles me,' Russell said. 'It's them big guns he's sporting. If we intend killing Scattergun Smith we'd best find ourselves a real safe place to do our shooting from.'

Dexter looked around them and pointed to an overhang.

'There!' he exclaimed. 'If we get ourselves up there he ain't got a snowball's chance in hell. It'll be a turkey shoot.'

Russell and Dexter raced towards the hardware

store's overhang. Like rats they clambered up the busted side wall and scrambled on to the flat overhang of the porch. Both men positioned themselves and waited with their .45s drawn and ready.

By the time Scattergun had travelled the length of the main street the storm had passed far away from the town and once again the sun was beating down upon its tormented ruins.

Debris littered his path as he pursued his hunt for the elusive outlaw. Lifeless bodies were scattered everywhere amongst the debris. He continued on his way towards the hotel.

His eyes searched the street, yet no matter how hard he tried Scattergun could not tell where the bodies of Black's cohorts had fallen. He had never seen such devastation as this. Personal belongings were mixed in with shattered woodwork and masonry across the entire street.

The hotel was still standing but its balcony had been torn from its frontage. Scattergun rested his wrists on the grips of his weapons and sighed heavily as he continued to make his way towards the hotel where, he was sure, Black and his cronies had rented a room.

As he cast his gaze from one hideous sight to the

next he suddenly became aware of something up high on the hardware store's overhang.

Although he could not see the pair of guards he knew that they were there, for the guns in their hands were flashing in the bright sunshine.

Scattergun stayed his progress. He was within range of their guns and was well aware he had to act quickly. He looked to either side of him.

An upturned trough offered him the best cover. More quickly than he had moved in the longest while, Scattergun drew the shotgun from his left holster and blasted one of its barrels up at the overhang. The sound of shattering window glass filled the street.

The instant the buckshot had left his weapon Scattergun threw himself across the intervening debris and landed behind the upturned trough.

He clambered back to his feet as a volley of bullets hit the underside of the trough, sending splinters flying in all directions. Scattergun replaced the spent cartridge.

As bullets ricocheted off the sturdy trough Scattergun remained behind its cover. He did not move until the shooting ebbed. Then he ran under the hardware store's overhang, aimed upwards and unleashed both barrels.

The buckshot pierced through the wooden boards above him as he dragged the other hefty weapon from its holster. Wood and sawdust rained down on Scattergun as he squeezed on his triggers again. Fiery rods of fury made the hole even bigger.

The sound of screams filled his ears as he swiftly expelled the spent shells from his weapons and reloaded.

Scattergun rested his back against the store's window and eyed the huge gap that he had created in the overhang above him. He could hear the groaning of the two men as blood dripped from the hole and made a crimson pattern at his feet.

'I ain't ever liked to hear critters suffer,' he whispered. 'Especially back-shooting critters.'

Scattergun raised one of his guns and pulled on his triggers. The hole above his head grew even bigger but the groaning ceased.

He holstered one of his shotguns and refilled the smoking chambers of the other as he walked to the edge of the boardwalk. He kicked at the upright and sent it flying. He had barely walked two yards away from the store when its own weight brought it crashing down to the ground.

Scattergun stopped and turned.

His eyes narrowed on the dead bodies that lay in pools of gore on the overhang. He dropped the smoking shotgun into its holster and shook his head.

'Who in tarnation were they?' he asked himself. 'Seems like every damn idiot with a gun is trying to kill me.'

Judge Cleveland Johnson had not made many mistakes in his profitable life, but he was about to make the most serious error of judgement anyone had ever made.

The sound of gunfire echoed around the town like the most stubborn of thunderstorms. Even the sturdy walls of his San Miguel home could not muffle it from the mine-owner's ears as he awaited the return of his guards.

Johnson downed a shot of whiskey and walked out into the sunshine. He had made his way out of the side door and down past his carriage when he realized that the gunfire had ceased.

The judge placed a cigar between his lips and waited for any sign of his men's return. He struck a match, lit the tip of his cigar and filled his lungs with its strong smoke. As the smoke filtered back through his lips he tossed the match aside and ventured closer to the outskirts of his property.

Johnson had not seen the hunched horseman hiding in the bushes ten feet from where he stood. Black tapped his spurs and straightened up as his grey walked slowly out into the street.

The judge touched the brim of his brown derby.

'Howdy,' he said innocently.

Black eased his reins back and studied the man who was sucking on a fine cigar. He tilted his head and then pulled a scrap of paper from his pocket.

Johnson looked up at Black as the outlaw read the note.

'What you got there, friend?' Johnson asked.

'Just a note,' Black replied. 'Reckon I got the right address.'

The judge was curious. He pulled the cigar from his mouth and stared at the rider astride the grey.

'You looking for someone in particular?' Johnson asked.

'You ever heard of a critter named Cleveland Johnson?' Black replied. He pushed the note back into his pocket. 'I hear he owns this house.'

The judge looked at Black. 'I'm Cleveland Johnson. Are you looking for me? What you want?'

Black drew and cocked one of his six-shooters. He aimed at Johnson and grinned.

'I don't want nothing,' he chortled. 'Just your hide.'

Black fired. The shot caught the mine-owner in his head. Johnson went flying backwards, the cigar falling from his fingers. Black turned and aimed his gelded grey in the direction of the livery stable. He spurred.

FOURTEEN

Scattergun turned away from his lethal handiwork and looked to the Long Branch. The saloon had fared better than most of the other buildings along the main street. Apart from a few broken window panes it had been virtually untouched by the wrath of the storm.

Scattergun walked cautiously to the saloon, stepped up on to its boardwalk and pushed the swing doors apart.

His eyes narrowed as he studied the patrons.

'Any of you critters seen Bradley Black lately?' he shouted loudly.

This time the customers shook their heads honestly.

The eerie sound of his spurs echoed around the interior of the saloon as Scattergun approached the bar counter. The two bargirls looked as though the violent storm had ruffled their plumage.

The rest of the saloon's customers looked little better.

Scattergun pulled a golden eagle from his pants' pocket and slammed it down on to the sand-covered counter.

'The drinks are on me, barkeep,' he drawled, 'and bring me one of them.' He pointed to what was left of the whiskey bottles.

Chuck the bartender picked up a bottle and placed it in front of Scattergun, looking at him nervously.

'Is that good enough for you?' he asked. He picked up the coin and tested it with his teeth.

'It'll do.' Scattergun nodded as he watched the storm battered men and women come slowly up to the bar for their free drinks.

The bargirls moved in on the heavily armed man.

'Ain't you found Black yet?' one of them asked. 'You sure ain't much of a bounty hunter.'

'I don't hunt bounty,' Scattergun told her and sighed.

146

'Then why do you wanna kill him for?' a voice piped up from the crowd.

Scattergun ignored the question, pulled the bottle's cork and took a swig from its neck. He sighed again and shook his head.

'I'm waiting for him to return,' he said.

'You must sure hate that critter.' The woman nearest him grinned as she accepted her glass of free liquor from the bartender. 'Anyone with sense would have high-tailed it out of town when the storm had passed, rather than wait for Black.'

'Does suicide run in your family, Mr Smith?' an elderly gent enquired.

'Not that I'm aware of, old-timer.' Scattergun took another swig of the fiery whiskey and turned to watch the swing doors.

The bartender, having given every one of his customers a free drink, now rested his hands on the counter by Scattergun.

'Black ain't in town,' he said.

'That's right. Black rode out before the storm got real ornery,' the other bargirl told Scattergun. 'We seen him pass.'

Scattergun frowned. 'Any idea where he was headed?'

A man with a bushy handlebar leaned close.

'He must have bin headed to General Cordova's place,' he said. 'That's the only spread in that direction.'

Scattergun raised an eyebrow. 'I seem to have heard that name before. Who exactly is this Cordova *hombre?*'

'He's a Mexican war hero, Scattergun,' the female closest to him said with a grin. 'Shucks, everyone knows that.'

'I didn't,' Scattergun admitted. 'Why would Black be headed there?'

'We get us a lot of dubious drifters in San Miguel,' a voice piped up.

'And they all seem to head off to the General's hacienda,' another voice added.

Scattergun turned and stared at them. 'These drifters wouldn't happen to be outlaws, would they?'

'We can't rightly say, but it sure seems likely,' the second bargirl said over her whiskey glass. 'Every damn stranger that rides into town always heads out to the hacienda.'

Scattergun took another long swallow from his bottle and pondered the notion of outlaws all heading to see someone who should not have anything to do with their breed of men.

148

'Why would they go to see Cordova?' he wondered aloud.

Chuck refilled a few of his customers' glasses.

'Maybe it's coz there ain't no law in San Miguel and it being so close to the border might have something to do with it, Scattergun,' he ventured.

Scattergun rubbed his jaw. 'It don't explain why Black and the others all go to see a respectable character like the General, does it?'

'It sure don't.'

'Maybe Cordova is a bandit?' someone suggested.

Scattergun exhaled. 'I kinda doubt a war hero is also a bandit. There has to be something else that's drawing them strangers to his hacienda. But what?'

There was no time for any of them to answer Scattergun's question. The swing doors burst open as the burly blacksmith came rushing into the saloon. Every eye in the Long Branch watched as Jeb Sharpe strode across the sawdust towards the bar counter.

'I figured I'd find you in here,' Sharpe panted. He rested one huge hand on the counter and stared at Scattergun.

'You look fit to burst, Jeb,' Scattergun said, lowering the bottle from his lips. He studied the red-faced blacksmith.

'I am,' Sharpe panted like an old hound.

'What's wrong, friend?' Scattergun handed the bottle to the blacksmith, who raised it to his mouth and drained a quarter of its contents before putting it down again.

'Black just rode back into town,' Sharpe told him. 'He brung his grey back to my livery. I reckon he's bin doing some killing 'coz there was smoke trailing from one of his holstered gun barrels.'

'How'd you get out of there without him seeing you leave, Jeb?' Scattergun asked.

'I used the side door and cut across my corral.' Sharpe replied. 'I run all the way here to warn you. He's gonna be mighty mad when he finds out what you done to his two friends, boy.'

Scattergun straightened up to his full height and pushed the tails of his long coat over his shotgun grips.

'I doubt if Black ever had any real friends in his entire life, Jeb,' he drawled. 'Those two young outlaws were just hirelings he'd picked up along the way.'

'But he'll be sore when he discovers they're dead, Scattergun,' Sharpe insisted. 'Real sore.'

'It'll pass when he's dead.' Scattergun drawled.

The patrons of the Long Branch had fallen silent as they listened to the two men discuss the infamous Black. They watched as Scattergun adjusted his shotguns and walked towards the swing doors and the sun-drenched street beyond.

The blacksmith watched Scattergun as he vanished into the sunlight. Sharpe turned and shook his head as his fertile imagination considered what was about to happen in San Miguel.

'There's a storm brewing,' he muttered.

'Where you bin, Jeb?' Chuck the bartender chuckled. 'The damn storm has come and gone.'

Sharpe's bloodshot eyes looked up at the bartender.

'Not by my figuring it ain't,' he said.

Scattergun placed a cigar between his teeth, struck a match with his thumbnail and brought it up to the black weed. He narrowed his eyes until they were focused on the livery stable at the far end of the long thoroughfare.

He blew out a line of smoke and extinguished the match.

The storm had left its mark. Nothing was how it had been when he had first ridden into San Miguel. Scattergun flicked the blackened match over his shoulder and walked towards the distant livery.

A trail of smoke drifted from his mouth and hung in the late afternoon sunshine. He tightened his gloves until they felt like another layer of skin. There was no sign of life anywhere around him.

Scattergun advanced closer to the large livery stables.

The storm had damaged and destroyed every building in the small town. The livery stable had not been spared its wrath.

Scattergun looked at the missing roof shingles and the gaps in its wooden walls. Somehow the ramshackle building had survived the storm's best efforts to rase it to the ground.

Coming within forty feet of the livery stable Scattergun stopped and rested his shoulder against a locked and shuttered doorway. He pulled the cigar from his lips and dropped it to the ground. He crushed its smouldering tip under his boot heel and rubbed his face.

His eyes were still focused on the livery stables and its open doors.

There was no sign of Black.

A thousand fleeting thoughts passed through his mind as he considered his options. He could call out and try to lure the devilish killer into the open, or he might just wait for Black to show himself.

Either way was as good or as bad as the other.

Countless other options flashed through his mind as he remembered why he had spent so long hunting the brutal and merciless killer.

Scattergun continued to stare at the livery as thoughts of his wife and child returned. He began to breathe faster as the terrible memories of their lifeless forms returned.

Black did not know it, but he had created Scattergun Smith.

Until the depraved outlaw had slain his beloved wife and daughter there had been no such creature. Scattergun had been created as a result of the outlaw's barbaric actions. Until then Scattergun had lived a normal life with his beautiful family. After the atrocity he had become the creature he now was.

For over a year Scattergun had been fuelled by revenge. He had become a hollow remnant of the man he used to be. All he had thought about since that fateful day was making Black pay the ultimate price for what he had done.

Long ago Scattergun had vowed to avenge his beloved wife and daughter and now that goal was within spitting distance. The hope of vengeance that had kept him alive this past year was about to be fulfilled.

There was no doubt in his mind that he would be triumphant. Good had to triumph over evil, didn't it?

Like an avenging angel Scattergun fearlessly moved away from the store front and walked towards the livery.

Suddenly Bradley Black's raised voice rang out. Scattergun stopped in his tracks for a heartbeat.

'Where the hell are you, Jeb?' the outlaw vainly shouted.

Scattergun leaned down and unhooked his vicious spurs from his boots. He pulled them free and discarded them, then straightened up.

'Where in tarnation have you gone, Jeb?' Black yelled again in the depths of the large livery.

Scattergun moved to the open doorway, inhaled deeply, then stepped silently into the livery stables and rested his back against one of the doors.

'Time to meet your Maker, Black,' Scattergun shouted at the top of his voice.

Two shots cut across the interior of the livery and knocked Scattergun off his feet. He fell backwards into the sunbaked street like a rag doll. A vicious pain in his chest racked him with agony.

Black raced across the dark interior of the livery towards Scattergun as he fell heavily on to the unyielding ground. More shots lit up the air and kicked up the sand on either side of him.

Scattergun rolled over and scrambled to his feet as another shot tore his Stetson from his head. He felt the drawstring snap under his chin as he fell beside a full water trough and took cover.

'Is that you, Scattergun?' Black yelled. 'About time you come close enough to die, boy.'

Somehow Scattergun managed to drag both his guns from their holsters and cock their hammers. Surrounded in gunsmoke, Black trained both his .45s on the trough and fired yet again.

The bullets hit the water and sent a wave over Scattergun. Quickly he lifted one of his shotguns and pulled on its triggers.

Two massive blasts spewed from his weapon's barrels.

Black retreated behind the tall stable door as it was peppered with buckshot. The door rocked on its hinges as its fabric absorbed the sheer power of the blasts.

Faster than the blink of an eye, Black fired again. The water inside the trough was kicked up over the figure now crouched behind it once more. Soaked to the skin, Scattergun looked around him, searching for a safer place to take cover. He ejected the spent shells, pulled two more from the crossed belts and pushed them into the smoking barrels.

He swung the hefty weapon until its barrels locked.

Scattergun was about to fire when he felt a dull ache in his chest again. He looked down and saw where Black's first shots had struck his crossed ammunition belts before ricocheting away.

'That was damn lucky!' he whispered.

Black swung around the edge of the livery door and fired his six-shooters to where he knew he had the legendary figure pinned down.

'Eat lead, you damn coward,' Black yelled, and laughed loudly. 'I'll teach you to lock horns with Bradley Black.'

Scattergun gripped his shotguns firmly and defiantly rose to his feet. He gritted his teeth and aimed both shotguns at the shaking livery door as Black took refuge behind it. There was a fire burning in Scattergun's guts. It burned every trace of fear from him.

With the shotguns held in both hands

Scattergun squeezed on all four triggers.

The combined fury of all four shotgun shells being fired at exactly the same time was devastating. A huge hole was punched through the barn door. Flesh, blood and bone erupted like a volcano from where Black had stood.

A blood-curdling scream echoed around the street outside. Scattergun strode towards the source of the terrible cry. He holstered one weapon and quickly replaced spent shells with fresh ones.

Scattergun aimed the fearsome shotgun at what was left of Bradley Black behind the shattered door. He lowered the shotgun and sighed. He had done what he had planned to do but felt no satisfaction at the horrific sight which greeted his eyes.

Scattergun slid the smoking shotgun into its holster as he heard the sound of horses behind him. He turned and saw that the two *vaqueros* were riding back towards Cordova's hacienda.

His eyes glanced at the remains of the outlaw again.

He said nothing.

FINALE

Sunset came as it always did and brought a chill to the desolate little town as the tall figure led his mustang from the livery stables and ran a gloved hand along its neck. Scattergun Smith gripped his saddle horn and stepped into his stirrup.

Jeb Sharpe watched as the younger man settled upon the saddle of his high-shouldered mustang and gathered his long leathers up in his hands.

'What's eating you, boy?' the blacksmith asked. He moved to stand beside the now rested horse and looked up at its master.

Scattergun glanced down at the stalwart man.

'I've bin hunting Black for the longest while, Jeb,' he said. 'I've trailed that stinking critter until I nearly forgot why I was after him.'

Sharpe nodded. 'I know, boy. You finally got him, though. Just like you said you would.'

Scattergun shrugged. 'Revenge drove me across deserts, swamps and forests. All I could think about was what that evil bastard did to my wife and daughter. All I could think about was making him pay.'

'You made him pay, boy.' The blacksmith nodded.

Scattergun forced a smile.

'I sure did.' He sighed. 'I made him pay, sure enough.'

Sharpe stared at the now moonlit face of the horseman.

'Then how come you look so sad, Scattergun?' he asked.

'I killed him but I don't feel any better for doing so, Jeb,' Scattergun admitted. 'Black deserved to die but I don't feel no satisfaction.'

'I didn't think you would.' The blacksmith smiled.

Scattergun turned the mustang and gazed up at the stars. He raised his hand in farewell. 'I'll be seeing you one of these days, friend. *Adios.*'

Sharpe watched as Scattergun galloped away from the small town. As the blacksmith turned he saw the discarded spurs on the sand. He grinned knowingly, then returned to his forge and his awaiting coffee pot.